THE BANDIT HUNTER

THE BANDIT HUNTER

by

Logan Stuart

Dales Large Print Books
Long Preston, North Yorkshire,
BD23 4ND, England.

British Library Cataloguing in Publication Data.

Stuart, Logan
    The bandit hunter.

    A catalogue record of this book is
    available from the British Library

    ISBN   1-84262-116-5 pbk

First published in Great Britain in 1957 by John Long Limited

Cover illustration © Prieto by arrangement with
Norma Editorial S.A.

The moral right of the author has been asserted

Published in Large Print 2001 by arrangement with
Roxy Bellamy, care of Watson Little Ltd.

Dales Large Print is an imprint of Library Magna Books Ltd.

Printed and bound in Great Britain by
T.J. (International) Ltd., Cornwall, PL28 8RW

CONTENTS

CHAPTER I

VENTURA

He reined in near to a low sandstone bluff, calculating how he would play this; weighing one alternative against the other with sober deliberation.

Both the man and the steel-dust were travel-stained and weary. It had been a long arduous chase, with little time for rest or refreshment over these last three days and two nights. But it looked like there would be plenty of opportunity to make up for those deficiencies right soon. Just as soon as Hank Dillis had been taken and delivered to the marshal at Latigos, Ventura could rest up all he needed; book a room for a week if needs be and sample the comforts of the Bosque House and maybe chance the wheel at the Trailsman saloon.

He rolled and fired a cornpaper quirly, allowing the smoke to drift from his aquiline nostrils, and the thought came to him, faintly disturbing, that a well-earned rest *could* be one of eternal duration!

Every town and frontier settlement had its boothill wherein lay the earthly remains of

9

others like himself, who had tried the same or a similar thing. His shoulders lifted in a gesture both fatalistic and self-derisive. *No importa!* A man might just as likely break his neck over a ravine, or stop a stray slug in a brawl; even lose his scalp to a party of Apache.

Ventura pulled the quirly from his mouth, wiped some of the sweat and alkali dust from face and neck and laid his gaze on the building barely visible beyond the sea of tawny buffalo grass. If it weren't for the fact that he had trailed Dillis here, likely he would have missed the house, half-hidden as it was in a stand of cottonwoods and juniper saplings. But over to the San Mateo range, the sun was westering beyond the snow-capped Cebolleta, its oblique rays throwing back a flare of light from a glazed window in the house.

And, across that sea of grass, a swathe had been made by a tired and lamed horse; Hank Dillis' horse, almost for sure. The man must have figured himself pretty safe by now and had cut straight across rather than risk his horse giving out, riding a wide half-circle.

Again Ventura fished the crumpled wanted notice from shirt pocket, pulling his gaze away from the lengthening shadows, to skim over the salient points. The dodger was issued from the sheriff's office at the county seat, but copies had been sent to all Law

Enforcement officers in the county, maybe even beyond. Ventura had assured himself on other such details before taking on what Marshal Will Baumann and his posse had succinctly described as 'a goddam, fruitless chore with not a single lead to go on!'

But Ventura had found a lead and had uncovered the trail. Maybe Hank Dillis had been in with the Butler gang on the bank hold-up at Plata or maybe not. Sufficient that the county was prepared to shell out $200 for the man's capture anyway, wanted as he was on two counts for robbery and one for a shooting. It could well mean one outlaw less, a red face for the marshal and – money was always a useful commodity. *Bueno!* He stubbed the cigarette butt on the saddle-horn, lifting the reins and gently rowelling the gelding forward in an un-compromisingly direct approach to the distant house, following the defined track of Dillis' mount.

For the first time, Ventura's compressed lips loosened in a meagre smile. Why should he decide to play it this way? Could be, he had an inherent dislike of creeping round to a man's back door even if that same hombre were a law-breaker. Too bad, if, instead of catching up on some of his lost sleep, Hank Dillis was even now watching from the tree-sheltered cabin, a carbine in his hands.

Ventura touched the six-gun at his side

11

and let his hand drop back lightly on his thigh. The *alamo* grove, with its scattering of junipers was perceptibly darker now as shadows lengthened over this high country. Already Latigos, in the Yerba valley six-seven miles northward, would be slowly coming to life; lamplight beckoning its nightly welcome to the town's saloons and deadfalls.

He kept the steel-dust to a walking gait and over the springing grass, iron shoes were no louder than muted drumbeats.

A wariness tightened the man's lean, sun-blackened face as horse and rider drew nearer to the house. He reached the scattered saplings, continued on, and shortly drew rein in the deep-cast shadow of a cottonwood. Shafts of sunlight slanted through the early summer foliage, striking patches of grass to create a dapple effect of light and shade. Yet, over the buildings hung an air of sombreness; loose boards and broken veranda rails adding to the per-vading atmosphere of neglect and deso-lation. There were no lights visible from behind the burlap-draped windows, and for the first time the thought entered Ventura's mind that the wanted man might somehow have gotten wise and out-foxed his trailer.

Beyond the barn, a small corral con-structed of unpeeled logs caught Ventura's raking gaze. But it was empty. If Dillis were in the house, likely then his horse would be either in the barn or around the back someplace.

Easily, noiselessly, the watching man stepped from leather, ground-anchoring the gelding before soft-footing over to the barn. He saw then the recently scuffed earth; shoe prints of a tired, limping horse, and the faint impression of high-heeled boots disappearing in the shadows towards the house.

The top half of the stable door stood ajar and Ventura, close in now, could hear the snuffling and pawing of Hank Dillis' saddler. And over the evening air, the sharp tang of ammonia-straw invaded his nostrils and drifted on to where the steel-dust stood cropping the grass beneath the tree.

He cursed as the gelding nickered sharply, its cry taken up and echoed softly by the stabled horse. He waited there, a slim-built, rawhide figure, silent and still, wondering if Dillis was in fact dead to the wide or whether those warning calls would reach down into the depths of his unconsciousness.

He remained there for perhaps five minutes, patient yet alert, as a hunter must be. At length, satisfied that his quarry would surely have made some sign before now, he began walking across to the house, careful as he ascended the steps to avoid rotting and broken planks.

As he touched the door latch, his eye caught a thin sliver of light escaping from between curtain and window frame. It could only be seen from this acute angle close to the door. Again he stayed put, considering briefly the possibilities of a trap. Almost imperceptibly he shook his head. He was pretty sure that if Dillis had gotten wise at some time over the last two days and a half, he would have doubled back on his trailer and laid for him. If not that, he would have waited in the shadow of the house or barn, gun in hand, ready to drop his pursuer at the ideal moment.

No! Having pulled their successful raid on the single bank at Plata, the Butler gang had scattered and, with their customary skill and luck, had thrown off all pursuit by Marshal Baumann's hastily mustered posse. It surely looked like Torch Butler's method was to pull a job and then for the gang to spread fast, each man taking a different trail, likely enough doubling back and confusing any sign before finally heading out for some isolated hideout and lying low for a while.

Ventura shrugged. What the hell did it matter which system Butler and his desperadoes used?

He tested the latch and surprise held him for a moment as the door moved to his touch. But rust-coated hinges suddenly shrilled their penetrating protest and on that instant, Ventura shoved hard, springing through and into the room beyond. He was aware of several things at once in the half light of a single, shaded table lamp. Most significant was Dillis himself, half-roused from the rumpled blankets on his cot; and in his right hand a long-barrelled gun, slanted upwards, the hammer not yet cocked!

So it was just like he had figured it, Ventura thought. It was not a trap; only the sudden, loud squeaking of the door had disturbed Hank Dillis' exhausted sleep.

He had ridden in unsuspectingly, likely enough real pleased with himself for making the roundabout trip to the cabin, confident no one was along his back-trail. Maybe he had arrived no more than a few hours back, had off-saddled and left hay in the manger for the weary bronc...

From the corner of his eye, Ventura had glimpsed the remains of a meal on the table, bread, opened cans and dirty plates, and he almost smiled at the pattern of things. A hastily wolfed meal, burlap curtains pulled and the lamp lit and turned low against the likelihood of the desperado's waking some time during the coming night!

Yet, despite the split-second of time lost over these realizations, Ventura's brain was the clearer and quicker of the two. He knew this for a certainty as he watched Dillis'

15

puffed eyes still half-muddied with sleep; not yet washed clear by the cold douche of complete comprehension.

'Who the hell are yuh, mister, an' what's the game, bustin' in on a man like this? Bigawd! yuh shore better make it good! Talk dam' yuh, afore I put a slug in yuhr belly–'

Another moment or two and Dillis' rudely awakened brain would be turning over with a smoother, faster precision.

Ventura smiled, relaxed and at ease save for the partially tensed muscles in legs and arms. His glance flickered over to one of the draped windows beyond the cot.

'All right, Jake,' he said softly. *'Take him!'*

Even had Dillis been dead sure, he could scarcely have risked ignoring that possible source of danger. Sure, it might be a trick, and not a new one at that, but there was a brash confidence in this stranger's attitude and a cool, sure light in his narrowed eyes. Dillis felt the sweat start from his brow and trickle down the matted sideburns. He became convinced he had heard the faint, metallic click of a gun being cocked. He swung his gaze away and over towards the window and knew at once that he had been bluffed as easily as any greenhorn. His eyes, bright now with fury, swivelled back to the intruder. A lance of flame, a gun's roar and hot lead searing his forearm, rendering the limb temporarily useless; a series of flashing

16

impressions so fast and close together that for a second, Hank Dillis could not believe the evidence of his senses.

But the long-barrelled gun slid from his grasp and crashed to the floor. The pain in his arm made him cry out and gunsmoke hung on the air thick now with silence and across from the cot the man still stood there almost as though he had never moved a muscle, except he held a smoking six-gun in his hand...

He opened his eyes, studied the rose-patterned wallpaper for a while and listened with half a mind to the sounds of life on the street and the subdued clatter of activity below him in the Bosque House.

Shortly, he arose from the brass-framed bed, pulled on trousers and boots and moved across to the washstand. He poured cold water into the basin, sluicing head, arms and upper body. From the blanket roll on the floor, he withdrew a razor and began the painful process of removing the four-day stubble of beard.

A half-hour later, in the restaurant, Ventura ate his noon meal, paid the waitress and made his way out on to the thronging boardwalk, turning down street towards the marshal's office. He was eight or ten paces from the jail when a democrat swerved on to Main from a side-street, bowling along at a fast lick. Even before wagon and team slowed to a stop in front of Sullivan's Mercantile, Ventura saw that the driver was a woman, and one of such surpassing beauty that it was like glimpsing some rare and fabulous jewel amidst a collection of geegaws and trinkets. He smiled thinly. Likely, the womenfolk of Latigos and the Yerba River valley would have something to say if such a comparison were voiced openly. Come to think of it, even in his three visits here, he had seen more than one pretty woman with bright eyes and soft-looking lips. Younger women these, whose skins were not yet burned and creased by sun and wind nor crow-footed around the eyes; whose mouths had not yet become compressed into thin, bitter slits by the rigours and hardship of frontier life over the years.

The waitress, Minnie, at the Bosque House; the schoolteacher whom some passer-by had greeted as Miss Randell, on Ventura's first visit; the girl with chestnut hair who worked in the Trailsman saloon – in a different social class perhaps – but pretty enough to attract most men.

He turned and sent his glance drifting across the street for a second time. This woman could not be without a deal of Spanish blood in her veins, he mused; not to look like that, the way she did. Her stetson, pushed back man-fashion, revealed the ink-

18

blackness and shine of her hair; it showed too, something of the high cheekbones, the short straight nose and dark-browed eyes.

He watched the graceful movement of her body as she set the brake and expertly hitched ribbons around the whipstock. For a moment, her face was angled away from him as she greeted someone on the board-walk. She straightened up, cast around for a shopping basket behind the wagon seat and sent her appraising gaze across to the opposite walk. He waited until her glance brushed him, cool as a desert breeze at night. Yet it seemed a soft interest touched her face for a moment and was gone before he could be sure.

Behind him, above the immediate sounds of talk and movement, a dry voice reached out.

'Not yore class, Ventura.'

He turned seeing Baumann in the door-way, and crossed into the office.

Will Baumann heeled the door shut, seal-ing off all but the more strident and pene-trating street sounds.

'Who is she?'

Ventura dropped his question into the pool of silence and, uninvited, dragged a windsor chair forward, easing himself down, one spurred boot braced against the law-man's desk.

Baumann regarded his visitor with barely

concealed distaste. 'Must you scratch all the dam' furniture when you come in here?'

Ventura fashioned and lit a quirly, carefully considering an answer to the question which he judged Baumann had intended to be either rhetorical or plain dam' provocative.

He cuffed back the dun-coloured stetson, moved his head slowly. 'It isn't the furniture I scuff, Marshal, it's your pride, and the hell of it is, you cain't afford to say what you think!'

Baumann's seamed face darkened. He tugged at his drooping moustache and transferred his attention to the littered desk, avoiding this dark-visaged rider's cold and level stare.

'You tell me, mister, jest why I cain't speak my mind,' he said softly, 'an' if it comes to that, what exactly *do* I think?'

'A man doesn't have to be a fortune-teller to see some things, Marshal. Like, for instance, the number of folk who hate the guts of a bounty hunter. Reckon mebbe that's about the one thing law-abiding citizens, Peace Officers an' outlaws all agree on, isn't it?'

Ventura blew a couple of smoke rings. 'A year back, Marshal, you'd never heard of me, but two times I brought in a wanted man whom the law couldn't grab–'

'Sure! An' two times you bin hard after the reward money–!'

20

'What's so bad about that? *You* get paid, don't you? No, the trouble is you're sore as hell, not only on account of the *dinero*, but because of what the mayor an' citizens may be thinking. It's like the scuffed-up furniture, only this time you're worried for fear that badge is getting scratched!'

Baumann gripped the edge of his desk until the sun-blackened fingers took on a bleached look.

'You better watch yore tongue, Ventura! You ain't liked very much around these parts an' you sure are right about that! The folks in Latigos is right behind me, an' that includes Mayor Jenkins–'

'…And the Spanish girl…?'

'You mean Miss Valdés? Why, sure! An' now you got the answer to yore first question, mebbe–'

Ventura stood up so suddenly that, almost, Baumann flinched. 'Let's put it that bounty hunters are not as popular as lawmen – or even outlaws!' He leaned across the desk, gazing down at the marshal from a face gone suddenly hard. 'But remember that every time a pelt is brought in, it means one skunk less. It means that some bank teller or express agent; some innocent bystander, mebbe, will go on being healthy 'stead of getting shot down and crippled or killed!'

Baumann stared. 'You sound like you–?'

Ventura stepped back, the tension flowing

from him as he dropped the cigarette butt and carefully trod on it.

'I was a lawman once–,' he began and suddenly closed his mouth tight shut.

Will Baumann fidgeted with the papers on his desk. He was beginning to see a little light in the darkness. Not much, but a flicker at least. He cleared his throat.

'Reckon I oughta be thankin' you fer bringin' in Hank Dillis last night. I was outa town, but my deputy, Ollie Kirby, told me–'

'Sure. I saw Kirby lock him up.' Ventura nodded towards the short passage leading to the four cells. 'Sounds a mite too quiet.'

Baumann said: 'I got back late. Ollie gave me yore note an' we tried questioning him.' The marshal shook his head. 'No dice! Kept his mouth shut tighter'n a clam. But we's dam' sure he's Dillis an' that he's one of Torch Butler's gang.'

'You've had him taken to the county town?'

'Sure. Ollie took him on the early stage this mornin', handcuffed! It's up to San Pablo now.'

'And is Kirby bringing the *dinero?*'

'Reckon so. But likely he won't be back before tomorrow night. You better stick around.'

Ventura nodded, moved across to the door as Baumann's voice, low-pitched, trailed after him.

22

'The "Spanish" girl as you call her is Judith Valdés, owner of Starcross. Or if you want it *hispano americano,* Señorita Judit Cuervo y Valdés...!'

Ventura's gaze raked the street, moving quickly over shaded plankwalks and sun-drenched lots. Neither way along Main was there any sign of the brightly painted democrat so far as he could see. He built a quirly and placed it between his lips and found cause enough in the situation to smile wryly at himself. Maybe a drink in the Trailsman would wash away such foolish notions, and he turned down past the Bosque House towards the saloon... How was she called? Judith! Judit Cuervo y Valdés, a lovely name for a lovely creature. And – what else had Baumann said? Had he not referred to her as the owner of a place called Starcross?

Some of the buildings in Latigos were of sun-warped timber; many, like the Bosque House and the Trailsman were built of thick adobe. But there was an added coolness in the atmosphere of the saloon and it had to do with the folk themselves. Nothing that a man could bite on, just a few faint in-dications; the turned head, the significant glance, the half-whispered comment, the lift of a percentage girl's bare shoulders. Thus had the news of Hank Dillis' capture travelled the rounds, and Ventura had little

23

doubt that with each telling some small yet salient detail had been added or maybe carelessly discarded altogether.

He swirled the whisky in his shot glass, gazing at the amber liquid thoughtfully. Maybe if he had told Baumann his story, Latigos and all the other two bit towns would have behaved a mite different. To hell with it! There were some things a man preferred to keep locked up inside him.

He was mildly surprised to feel the touch of a hand on his arm; not nervously light, nor yet over heavy with belligerence. His glance swung round to rest on a pleasant-faced young man with sun-darkened skin, ink-black hair and rather surprisingly blue eyes. He was beardless, but broad sideburns almost reached to the ends of his long, carefully trimmed moustache.

'Have a drink with me, Ventura!' He placed a silver piece on the polished counter and the barkeep flicked it up. 'Thanks, Mr Valdés,' he grinned.

'Valdés, huh?'

'Permit me to introduce myself, Mr Ventura. Esteban José Cuervo y Valdés, at your service!'

'Of Starcross?'

The man's eyes widened a fraction. 'You know me then?'

'No-o.' Ventura smiled briefly. 'Just that a Miss – or should I say – Señorita Valdés was in town a while back. Someone mentioned her name; that she was owner of a place called Starcross, a *rancho* mebbe?'

Valdés frowned. 'Ah, my sister, señor. But you were perhaps only half informed. You see, we *both* own Starcross. But tell me about this – this capture of yours – please do not misunderstand me,' Valdés continued hurriedly as he noted the other's sudden chill expression.

'The Valdés family are not curs who run snapping and barking at the horses' hooves! Maybe you know, Señor Ventura, or at least have guessed, that such incidents as the capture of a bandit are far from common-place in a town like Latigos. Furthermore, I seem to recall that such a thing happened about a year ago, maybe less. And this strange name of yours – Ventura...' He smiled again and lifted his broad shoulders in an expressive gesture. 'Fortune! It rang a bell in my mind when I heard it again!'

Ventura regarded his polite inquisitor with a mixture of irritation and mild curiosity. Why should the fellow single him out and ask for the story, such as it was, of the taking of Hank Dillis? Maybe, Valdés didn't have any reason other than a simple desire to be friendly. Certainly within the last few minutes, the atmosphere in the Trailsman had undergone a subtle change. Whilst the customers were careful not to stare, they

25

were no longer *avoiding* Ventura's eyes; there seemed a lessening of hostile reserve, and as his glance lifted to the girl at the roulette wheel, Ventura acknowledged the faint, welcoming smile on her vivid lips.

It looked like this Esteban Valdés was kind of blazing a trail which the others, or most of them, were willing to follow. But who the hell cared what Latigos or the Yerba Basin thought, anyway? Let them figure things whichever way they chose.

'Maybe,' Valdés murmured, 'you would care to ride back with me to Starcross? You have a little time to kill, *si*?'

Ventura finished his drink, slid a *peso fuerte* over the counter and half-filled both shot glasses from the bottle at his elbow. He shoved Valdés' glass across, considering the invitation, and on to the retina of his mind flashed the picture of an olive-skinned girl, hair shining black as the shimmering plumage of a raven, mobile mouth soft and red like a cornfield poppy... He heard himself replying in the Border lingo *'Gracias, amigo!* As you say, I have a little time to kill...!'

CHAPTER II

STARCROSS

Charlie Williams leaned against the corral fence, to all outward appearances a perfect picture of absolute indolence. In emphasis of this, he drew a block of tobacco from the pocket of his ancient brush jacket, cut a thin slice and shoved it in his mouth, working his jaws with a steady rhythmic gusto.

If his body were not directly engaged in active work, his brain was busy, and the blue eyes which surveyed the world from a saddle-leather face were brightly restless.

Maybe if Glenville Summers, the *segundo*, were around, Charlie might make some kind of a showing, strictly for Miss Judith's sake. And the same principle operated for Esteban, except of late, he was more often away than at home.

Charlie shifted the quid to the other side of his mouth, blue eyes on the dirt road ahead. For a couple of miles or so it showed clearly, before dropping down from Mesa level and winding on for a further two miles to Latigos.

She sure ought to be back by now, he

mused, and figured the time at around three o'clock. Had anyone told Williams he was stewing, and in fact always did when Judith Valdés drove out alone, he would have scornfully refuted the idea.

A few cattle drifted over the far buffalo grass, ambling their way across the dirt road, likely heading for the creek. A thin dust-cloud appeared, and immediately the oldster identified the bowling democrat and team.

In a little while he was sure about the driver, and now he waited out the time until Judith swung team and wagon into the wide yard fronting the ranch buildings. As she approached the white adobe house, the wrangler moved across to the hitching rail. 'You bin gone longer'n you figgered, Miss Judith!'

She heard the implied accusation; it was there in the very inflexion of his voice, and she smiled softly, understanding more than anyone else the reason for it.

'I'm sorry, Charlie. It wasn't that there was a great deal to do. I guess maybe I delayed rather in Miss Finch's shop...'

Williams grinned. 'You got yourself a new dress, mebbe?'

'I – I – well, yes, Charlie, I have. I guess I shouldn't have spent the money...'

'Why not; it's yours, ain't it?'

She arose from the wagon seat, accepting

his proffered hand and stepped lightly to the ground.

'You be needin' the wagon again, Miss Judith?'

'No, Charlie. See to the team, will you? And while I remember, Mr Holman will be visiting this evening.'

'Holman, huh?' He shot the girl a quick glance.

'Ah, I know how you think of Roy – of Mr Holman – and the Arrow *rancho*, but please, for my sake, think much but say little. He – it may be that he – Roy – will…'

'You – you ain't figgerin' on gettin' a proposal?'

She smiled gently, searching for prosaic words. 'You are – how they call a dyed-in-the-wool bachelor – *un soltero*, Charlie!' She nodded towards the ancient house with its unpainted shutters, its air of neglect.

'We are not raising enough money to keep this old *casa* going – and besides, I do not believe marriage is as bad as you imply.'

'Mebbe so, but not with Holman. Why he's–'

Judith loosened the rawhide plaited chin strap, pushed the dusty stetson far back so that it rested between her shoulder blades.

'What is he?' she asked softly, 'and why do I waste valuable time listening to your grumbles, Señor Williams?'

'The answer to the second part is on

29

account you're who you are – Judit Cuervo y Valdés,' Charlie said simply. 'You cain't have any explanation better'n that!

'As for Holman, why, ain't it a fact which most everyone knows, he's kinda power-crazy! More dinero, more land and as if that ain't enough, angling for to become a territorial leader.'

'Perhaps it would not be an unpleasant position to be the wife of a territorial legislator, even one day to become the governor's lady?'

He looked at her out of his nut-brown wrinkled face, shaking his head solemnly.

'It ain't what you want, Miss Judith, I'll bet on that. Ain't there some other way we kin raise some *dinero*? Sure, I know we lost three hun'ed head' – the oldster raised his clenched fists in quick anger– 'Prime stuff, all set fer hazin' to Fort Frazer the next day.'

She said softly, 'And in the morning, the whole gather bloated and dying, fed on locoweed and no sign of either Jack or Red Fletcher!'

'They wasn't the brains, Miss Judith. You know that! Neither them Fletcher kids had the savvy to think up a trick like that, but *I* got an idea who–'

'Please, Charlie! We can't make accusations without any proof or evidence and if *we* could not find any clues beyond a few shoe-prints, then we could not expect the law–'

'What about the Butler gang?' Williams obediently switched his train of thought away from Roy Holman and Arrow.

'Why, Charlie, I had almost forgotten to tell how the town was buzzing this morning. I heard it first at Sullivan's. One of the Butler desperadoes was caught last night, I think they said–'

'Who was it, Miss Judith?'

'A man called – Dillon? No, Dillis!'

'Hank Dillis,' Charlie nodded. 'I mind the talk about him. The law allus figgered he wasn't so close to Torch Butler like some of the others. But there was sure a reward notice out. How come Will Baumann managed to bring him in so long after the hold-up at Plata's bank?'

'He didn't, Charlie. Leastways, it wasn't the way I heard it!'

'Then mebbe the sheriff's posse from San Pablo...?'

She shook her head. 'Mr Sullivan was talking about it amongst two-three other customers when I entered the Mercantile. But I – I think I saw the man who...' Judith Valdés' words trailed off. Her gaze had been on the dusty yellow ribbon which was the trail to town. Two riders were briefly sky-lined before their trotting mounts left the dip behind them, and Williams' bright eyes swivelled round, following the direction of Judith's glance.

'One's sure enough Esteban,' he grunted, 'but who in hades he got with him? No one as I kin recognize!'

'Wait!' She turned and sped across the flagged *pavimento* to the doors and entered the cool interior, scarcely aware that she was so breathlessly making haste, or even why.

She found the army glasses within a few seconds, and over the *pavimento* her high-heeled Justins beat a quick and urgent tattoo.

'I cain't figger it,' Charlie grunted, a calloused hand shading his eyes from the glare of the westering sun. 'It shore ain't Holman nor Glen...'

He heard her swift intake of breath and swung his head round. She was holding the glasses steady on the still distant riders, but magnification rendered every detail clear and unmistakable. Where, before, Judith Valdés had no more than sensed something faintly familiar, she was now quite sure. There could be no gainsaying the evidence brought to her in such sharp focus. It was the man with whose steady eyes her own glance had locked, just for that moment before she had descended from the wagon and entered the store. But there was more to it than that. Folk in town had called him the bounty hunter, the man who had brought in one of the Butler gang. Had not they also referred to some such similar incident way back, and described this man...? She recalled the Señor Sullivan's remark as she had threaded a way to the counter: *Sure, that's the fellow, Henry, just gone into the marshal's office!*

'I saw him for the first time today,' Judith murmured, 'for perhaps four-five seconds and *this* is the one who captured the outlaw, not Baumann!'

'Then he's the hombre who pulled it off before! I mind how he rode circles round the posses an' left 'em all with red faces. The fella calls himself – wait a minute – Ventura! Yeah.'

'Ventura! Ah, yes. Yet he is *Americano!* Look for yourself, Charlie!'

He took the proffered glasses and after a moment lowered them, nodding slowly.

'Now I see him close up through them spy glasses I kin remember... But why you suppose yore brother's bringin' him here, Miss Judith; most gen'rally folks don't cotton on to scalp hunters?'

'*Quién sabe?* Maybe we shall find out later. Maybe not. Meanwhile I have to tell Carlotta there will be another guest tonight.'

Charlie watched her disappear into the house before climbing to the democrat's seat and driving over to the wagon shed.

Judith sat before the wrought silver mirror, pausing every few moments as she brushed her shining black hair. Any other woman, she told herself, particularly the mistress of a *rancho*, would be hastening to receive an arriving guest – even a bounty hunter! Instead of which, here she was unhurriedly making her toilette, deliberating with half her mind which gown to wear and which of the few remaining pieces of jewellery would be most suitable for the occasion. She must not forget, however, that the Valdés' guest tonight was not primarily a wandering, grubline rider with a dark handsome face; but a powerful and wealthy *ranchero*, a man of substance, integrity and foresight. Integrity? She threw the word out, too strict with herself to tolerate hypocrisy even in thought.

Voices drifted faintly over the evening air from the direction of the low walled yard, and suddenly Judith Valdés laughed softly at her reflection in the mirror. What reason had she for believing Ventura would stay long enough to avail himself even of a supper invitation?

Maybe Esteban had brought him out here merely to see a horse or a Spanish pistol from the armoury cabinet. Maybe he was the kind of man who always felt awkward and ill at ease even in such an informal atmosphere, preferring to take a cup of coffee and a sandwich at the kitchen table.

Quickly she arose and moved across to the

34

open windows at the far end of the room. She pushed one of the angled shutters to gain an unrestricted view of the scene below, seeing Esteban and the man Ventura stepping from their saddles as Charlie came forward from the shadows of the outbuildings.

'The Señor Ventura will be stopping over for a while, Charlie,' Esteban told the wrangler. 'See that both the horses are stripped and cared for.'

'Sure.' Williams stepped forward, a grin on his walnut face. 'But fust off I'd sure admire shakin' hands with the hombre as pulled in Hank Dillis.'

Ventura returned the old man's handclasp, smiling briefly. 'News travels fast. How did you know?' Two men here, Ventura considered, with opposing outlooks, even though they were both Starcross. Yet each one had extended him a friendly welcome in their different ways.

He did not miss the swift flash of anger in Valdés' eyes as the man's gaze moved over Williams, and again a mild curiosity nudged Ventura. There was something vaguely puzzling, even contradictory, in the set-up at Starcross, yet it might well be nothing more than an oldster's almost natural resentment against the new-fangled notions of a later generation.

'Miss Judith was in town today,' Charlie

35

said, speaking quickly. 'An' I reckon most folks was doin' their share o' gossipin'.' He caught Esteban's eye. ''*Stá bien, jefe,* I'm on my way!'

They watched him gather up the reins and lead the horses past the *pavimento* and across the yard.

'He's been with us a long time,' Valdés explained with a smile and a shrug and started towards the house. 'First I think we need to wash off the dust–'

'Wait.'

Esteban turned at the other's mildly uttered command. '*Qué pasa?*' he asked. 'What is the matter?'

Ventura indicated his trail-stained clothes and removed his stetson, cuffing it against his legs and raising a small dust cloud.

'Mebbe there's a place to wash up in back of the bunkhouse yonder?'

Valdés nodded. 'Sure, but you – you are...'

'...Your guest, Valdés? Sure, and I appreciate your hospitality, but I wouldn't want Miss Judith to take one look at me and run!'

'Have it your way, Ventura,' the Starcross man grinned. 'I'll show you the way.'

Still screened by the half-open shutters at her bedroom windows, Judith had ample opportunity for studying the 'mysterious' stranger. She could not help thinking of him in that way, for it seemed so very little was known about him as yet. Even the name was unusual enough to be assumed, but perhaps before the evening was through, she would learn something about this slim, yet powerful-looking man. And if she were really honest about the matter, then acknowledge she must, that other factors contributed towards her quickening interest; factors clearly discernible and not vague impressions to be guessed at. The lean, sunburned face; the pale yellow hair which the sun's oblique rays now touched with the shine of corn-silk; the deep-set, steady eyes whose colour as yet she could not have determined. And beyond those things, a quality seen only by those with eyes to see. A *pride*, perhaps in himself or in his forebears, maybe in his own quiet strength or prowess...

She pulled back from the window and began to dress her hair before the mirror. *Bounty hunter, drifter, saddle-tramp!* her thoughts kept on saying. So utterly different from a man like Roy Holman, who, for all his faults and maybe vices, yet sank his foundations firm and built on steadily towards the attainment of his goal.

Deftly she wound the long coil of hair, fastening it into a knot at the nape of her neck, sat regarding her dwindling array of dresses. Sometimes it could be almost amusing to spread them all out, even the tarnished and moth-eaten ones, and then deliberate over the final choice as though style and finery were the only considerations! But of late it had become a matter of merely deciding between two; one, a black laced Spanish gown, the other a flame-coloured dress threaded at the neckline with black silk ribbon and tiered from the tight waist downwards in a full series of black-edged flounces. Roy liked this one especially.

She smiled enigmatically, reaching for the box which Carlotta's daughter Josefa had carried in, and withdrew the new dress so cleverly copied by Miss Finch from a San Francisco ladies' journal. She ran her fingertips over the deep purple velvet, deriving a half-sensuous, half-ethereal pleasure from its peach-soft texture. Then abruptly she moved across to the bell cord...

A half-hour later, Judith Valdés descended the curving staircase, pausing a moment to return Josefa's quick smile before the Mex girl pattered away to the rear of the house.

There was no sound of voices downstairs and, as Judith stepped into the living-room, she discovered that only Ventura was there, standing before the huge stone fireplace and gazing straight into her eyes.

'Your brother has just stepped outside, Miss Valdés, to welcome a – a Mr Holman, I reckon he said. But mebbe you don't know who...?'

'I know you are the Señor Ventura,' she smiled slowly, crossing towards him. 'And that you rode in with Esteban a while back. Welcome to Starcross!'

'*Gracias.*' He took her outstretched hand with a marked courtliness. 'Seems to me, Miss Valdés, that you and I have met up some place before!'

His tone was deadly serious, but she caught the sudden brightness in his grey eyes and laughed full-heartedly.

'Would it have been on Main of a town called Latigos?' she quipped, turning to a *cajonería* on which stood a decanter of wine with an array of crystal glasses.

He watched the play of light and shade on shapely arms and shoulders, admiring the sideways tilt of her head, the graceful curve of her breast. The faintest tinge of madder stained her cheeks as she set down the decanter and proffered a glass.

'You like my dress, Mr Ventura?' She met his gaze squarely, deep blue eyes filled with a sober interest despite the banter in her voice.

'You are beautiful,' he said softly, and suddenly switched his glance to the man at the door.

From that first moment of meeting, and throughout the meal, it was plainly evident to Ventura that this Holman hombre was a mite annoyed; and very gradually from the cross-channels of talk with their occasional innuendoes, Ventura's mind began to form a clearer picture. The more he considered one particular aspect of the set-up the more certain he became of several significant truths.

He was no stranger to this kind of *rancho,* whose grazing lands and water rights had so often been originally acquired under Spanish grants; *ranchos* whose buildings and wealth had decreased over the years for any of a score of different reasons, and for all the extravagant size and design of the Valdés *casa,* the light of failure, of fast-diminishing wealth became apparent after a while. The only servants here seemed to be the woman Carlotta and her daughter. The brocades and tapestries might have cost a king's ransom years back. Now many of them were hanging almost threadbare.

Here and there over the stucco walls were lighter patches, faint, yet clear enough to suggest that shields and swords had proudly hung there once. And outside, Ventura's raking gaze had not missed such small yet suggestive signs as crumbling adobe and weather-worn ironwork and timber.

Added to these outward indications, were the occasional significant word or phrase, dropped especially by Holman whenever an opportunity showed. Thus, the broad outlines and masses of the picture materialized before Ventura's eye, and anger stirred deep down within him as Holman cleverly and subtly offered his wealth and power against the gracious loveliness of Judith Valdés. And here, obviously, was the reason for the Arrow owner's ill-humour; the fact that a drifting saddle-tramp should be present, when according to all expectations, this should have been an intimate 'family' affair.

As for Esteban, he was more subdued than he had been ever since meeting Ventura in the Trailsman. For the most part intent on his food, yet throwing in an occasional droll remark; reserved, but seemingly by his expression, in quiet good humour.

Presently Holman pulled his gaze away from Judith, turning his sloe-black eyes on Ventura. One huge hand remained half covering the girl's bare arm as though, Ventura thought, to establish undisputed claim. With his left hand he caressed the long, silky moustache covering his upper lip, elbow braced firmly on the table.

'Esteban here was tellin' me you was the hombre as rounded up that outlaw Dillis. That right, mister?'

Valdés glanced up sharply. He had figured on getting the story from Ventura after supper, maybe when Judith and Roy were out on the moonlit *patio* together. But now that Holman had jumped in, this might be the only chance of getting Ventura to talk!

41

'Sure he is, Roy,' Valdés chipped in. 'Señor Ventura agreed to tell us the whole story in return for his supper, you know? Like the travellers of old.'

'I guess I forgot to bring my geetar with me,' Ventura smiled. But it was a cold sort of smile, Judith observed, and realized that Esteban's puerile joke had, in the way with children's humour sometimes, become a barb, a barb that had pierced this stranger's pride.

She was thankful that for the moment Roy's meaningful gaze no longer crawled over her. She could study Ventura in more detail, intrigued at the suggestion of latent strength and purpose beneath his façade of calm. Even the massive Holman in his tailored broadcloth suit and custom-made boots did not seem quite so menacing as he sought to batter down Ventura's gaze, only to finish by shifting his own.

Ventura said mildly, 'In my books the travellers usta tell their stories on account they were usually a mite short on gold! How much you figger, Esteban...?' His good-humoured laugh softened the near insult, and only Judith saw that this man could play both her brother and Roy Holman at their own game. But at least Esteban acknowledged the thrust with a quick flush to his face. Holman looked mystified and fished in his pocket for a cigar, and Judith gently sighed her relief as the Arrow owner's sweaty hand left her arm.

'How come you was able to pull somethin' neither o' them two posses could?' he asked, holding a match to the cigar and blowing great clouds of smoke across the table. He showed big yellow teeth in a grin intended to be disarmingly friendly.

'There wasn't a great deal to it,' Ventura said slowly. 'It happened I found something which the law must've overlooked at Plata. There seemed to be evidence enough that the hold-up was planned and carried out by the Butler gang, but no one seemed to know which particular men took part.'

'You mean,' Esteban said, 'that the job bore the earmarks of Torch Butler, but no one identified any actual individuals?'

'Something like that.' Ventura spoke quite casually, as though he were recounting a simple, everyday incident. 'Sometime after the robbery, I cut sign; it looked promising–'

'*Por qué?*' Valdés asked. 'How come?'

'I recognized the horse shoes, or at least one of them. After that it was just a question of following the tracks for two-three days!'

Holman frowned, then guffawed mightily as if he had heard just about the funniest thing ever.

'Don't sound easy to me!' he grinned. 'Whaddya say, Steve? Reckon you an' me could foller hoss sign plumb all over fer three days – huh?'

Esteban fingered his well-trimmed moustache, glanced from one to the other with slightly raised brows. 'I guess it would take a first-class tracker to do a job like that, Roy.' His blue eyes shifted back to Ventura. 'But that's not the end of the story! Where did you find this Dillis hombre and how did you take him?'

'Maybe Mr Ventura considers that is his own private affair,' Judith said quietly.

'Ah!' Holman splashed more wine into his glass and downed it with noisy gusto. 'A kinda trade secret, you mean, Jude?'

Not for the first time did Ventura wonder how such a loud-voiced, boisterous character could have walked in on them so quietly at the beginning. He shrugged, anxious now to have done with the recital. 'A lonely cabin in the trees, a travel-weary horse in the barn, tracks – what else would you expect to find but an exhausted man asleep on his cot?' It all sounded so easy, just as Holman had said earlier. They were not sure now whether to nod sagaciously or just express a smiling scepticism. Ventura had them cleverly balanced on the edge, especially Esteban; even the Arrow man was nonplussed for a while. Only the girl's deep blue eyes stared straight back, carrying a smile of warmth and respect...

CHAPTER III

THURSDAY RENDEZVOUS

All morning, Dulcie Randell had struggled to keep her attention on the children in the classroom and her mind on the lessons. Now and again, in spite of stern efforts to the contrary, she found her thoughts slipping away, hurrying on ahead so that just for a moment it would seem as though the afternoon had truly arrived and she was on her way to that secret trysting place at once so lovely and yet so sad.

Once, however, she had convinced herself that the clock hands must surely have stopped moving and that there was no point, therefore, in watching any more, her mind became more fully absorbed with subject and pupils alike. She really did love her job, even though it was often enough slow, uphill work. And sometimes she would feel a swift surge of pride after some particular fragment of knowledge had been hammered home to achieve a more or less satisfactory degree of success.

It was the pert little Jenny Rawlins who, having recently mastered the art of time-telling, shot up her hand at that moment, quite decided in her own mind that ten minutes' grace was time enough to give anyone.

'Yes, Jenny, what is it?'

'Please, Miss Randell, it's – it's *already* near a quarter after noon...!'

With mingling expressions of relief and apology on her pleasant face, Dulcie Randell dismissed the class, remaining quite still at her desk until the human tornado in miniature had swept from the room to a rising crescendo of shrieks and squeals of delight.

Today was Thursday, and that meant school was finished until nine o'clock the next morning. No wonder the kids were high-spirited; bodies and strident voices suddenly released like corks from a champagne bottle!

And, as it was also the last Thursday in the month it meant a freedom for Dulcie Randell more deeply significant than a mere break in the routine of school. A release was it? she asked herself with a wistful smile. No, not exactly; rather more a kind of parole where the prisoner is allowed a purely *temporary* concession on account of good behaviour. She glanced down at the gold band encircling the third finger of her left hand. Well, she *had* to maintain her good behaviour so long as she wore this solemn

46

symbol, and it was too late in the day now, to discard it; at least so far as the Yerba Valley was concerned and in particular, the town of Latigos.

She gathered up her books from the desk, tied them firmly with a strap before donning her lace shawl and brightly trimmed, grey bonnet. Maybe she had been a fool in the first place to have continued wearing the ring. By what right did a drunken wastrel like Sam Fredericks continue to demand money, to threaten–? She stopped herself in mid-stream. Would it have made any difference? Sam had found out where she had gone, either through his misguided shrewdness or else by sheer chance.

As for his rights... Momentarily, Dulcie Randell's face assumed an expression of un-utterable bitterness. Had he not the rights of any lawful husband, which too often included a denial of all responsibilities?

Abruptly she stepped from the school-room, locking the door and hastening across to the small adobe cottage which the citizens of Latigos had provided for their first official school teacher.

Inside the kitchen-parlour, Dulcie dropped the books on to a chair before opening up the stove's damper and setting coffee to boil. She had little enough appetite today, but stubbornly she ploughed her way through a hunk of cold meat and some home-baked bread, afterwards pouring out the warm coffee, stirring in cream and sugar.

She moved across to a mirror and stood regarding her reflection quizzically, seeing an oval, sun-tanned face with clear grey eyes and short, finely chiselled nose. Her mouth was generously wide, inclined to an attractive fulness and the dark-honey hair was drawn back behind her ears to the point of severity.

Perhaps she might even look beautiful if she tried, and she examined this thought objectively and without any trace of vanity. But with her hair styled in the height of eastern fashion and rouge for her lips, she might well forfeit such respect as Latigos accorded her – even to the extent of jeopardizing her job and livelihood.

Tongues had clacked quite enough when she had first arrived, quickly confessing that although she was married as evidenced by the ring, she preferred to be known and addressed by her maiden name.

Thus had Dulcie contrived not to lie, yet had omitted many details which she had intuitively known would ostracize her if repeated in a place like Latigos.

She turned back to the table, finished the now cool java and prepared quickly for her expedition...

Always on Thursday afternoons Hatch Nimrod had a rig ready and waiting for the school teacher who liked to spend her free afternoon driving around. According to Miss Randell herself, she would sometimes drive over to Plata to see an ageing aunt. Other times, maybe, it would be San Pablo, ten miles distant and seemingly it would take most of her time just to get there and back before dusk. There was no doubt in the hostler's mind that Miss Dulcie liked driving a buckboard just for the hell of it; and if such weekly sashayin's had lifted eyebrows amongst the traders' wives at first, then the thing had by now become an accepted routine.

Certainly Dulcie Randell *did* visit around quite a bit as other folk could tell. But no one had ever seen her in San Pablo or Plata or along the Griffin homestead on the last Thursday of the month and not surprisingly, no one had ever thought twice about it...

She made her way along the walk, acknowledging an occasional smile or quickly fingered sombrero and halted just inside the livery barn.

Hatch Nimrod had but this moment harnessed the bay and hitched it to the buckboard. He straightened up at the sound of her step and touched his hat, smilingly.

'All set fer yuh, Miss Dulcie, whenever yuh're ready. Wh'ar yuh figgerin' on headin' today?'

'Oh, I – I did think of driving along by the

river for a way. Maybe find myself a real quiet spot some place and – do a little reading!' She withdrew a book from the basket on her arm and Nimrod peered through his steel-rimmed spectacles, reading with slow deliberation. '"The Complete Works of Shakespeare," huh?' The old man grinned. 'Reckon yuh shore have more'n a afternoon's readin' there, Miss Dulcie. Don't yuh go forgittin' the time now, an' be keerful–'

'Careful, Hatch, of what?'

'Waal, we ain't got all that much law around these parts. Reckon yuh done heard that only last night thet bounty hunter captured Hank Dillis–'

'I did hear talk of it this morning, Hatch, but I've been real busy on a new curriculum for the children – I guess I didn't pay much attention. But, if the thief or whatever he was has gotten himself taken what is there to worry about? In any case, *I* have no valuables – or anything–'

'Yuh ain't bin here so very long, Miss Dulcie, an' I reckon apart from the bank hold-up at Plata, things has bin middlin' quiet for a spell.'

'Well, then–?'

Nimrod shoved his hat to the back of his head and laid his gentle gaze on the girl.

'Runnin' a livery stable, a man gits to hear quite a few things. Sure, mebbe most of it is gossip an' half-truths. But riders come in now and again an' drop a word here an' there– Another thing. Thet hombre Dillis as was brought in an' then hauled off to San Pablo, why he sure enough is reckoned to be one o' Torch Butler's gang–'

'But I told you,' Dulcie smiled. 'I don't possess anything of value to robbers and road-agents even – even if I ever did meet up with any of this – this Butler gang!'

'Yuh're a purty woman, Miss Dulcie, an' they's men around these parts as wouldn't think twice – I reckon I'm old enough by sixty-odd years to talk thisaway to yuh. So yuh won't be thinkin' bad of me when I say that *dinero* and jewels ain't the only things some o' these *mal hombres* figger worth takin'!'

She could not stop the colour flowing into her cheeks, and laid her hand on Nimrod's arm. 'How could anyone think badly of you, Hatch? And besides, I am grateful for your warning.' She stepped across to the rig, placing the napkin-covered basket carefully under the seat and turned back to face the liveryman. For a moment she wavered in her resolve to conceal the truth from everyone including Nimrod. The oldster had shown a sympathetic concern for her almost from the start and at moments like this, she experienced a feeling of obligation towards him – almost as though she were in his debt.

51

Perhaps this was what real friendship meant, anyway; each person indebted to the other by reason of a mutual trust and loyalty offered without conditions.

But there was Mike to consider; Mike Santeely who had dreams and ambitions and whose roots were sunk pretty deep right here in the Yerba Valley!

'I have seen some of the rougher sides of life, Hatch,' Dulcie Randell smiled, 'even back in Iowa. But,' – she gathered her skirts and stepped nimbly into the buckboard before ever Nimrod could offer his hand– 'I promise to look out for myself, Hatch, and thanks again for your … help.'

He grinned and stood back from the runway, approving the way in which she held the bay on a firm yet gentle rein, and watched from the doorway as the buckboard turned on to Main.

Near to the old *plaza* was the Express Stage Office, and here Dulcie pulled in, hitched the reins and climbed down. The noon-day coach from San Pablo had long since arrived and departed and likely there had been the usual mail sacks aboard.

A small crowd was gathered inside and when it came to the school teacher's turn, Billy Sharples handed her a single envelope, before turning to the next one in line.

She knew the writing well enough. That flourishing scrawl was unmistakable even

52

though the postmark was a trifle blurred. But she had scarcely hoped for any mail apart from Sam's letter and she felt no extremes of either pleasure or disappointment. Doubtless this was a replica of other half-pitiful, half-threatening pleas for money, and hurriedly the girl tucked the letter into her picnic basket under the seat and set off ostensibly towards the distant line of green, marking the Yerba River.

Some two miles out of town, she swung the buckboard from the stage trail on to a level stretch of timbered parkland. She was now heading westward and roughly parallel with the river instead of towards it.

Lance-leaved cottonwoods and willows gave way to scattered juniper stands as the land rose in a series of grassy mesas slashed by shallow canyons and dry washes. Twice during the first hour's hard driving, Dulcie Randell drew into the shade of an overhang to rest the sweating horse and ease her own aching arm muscles. On this second occasion, she remembered Sam's letter and reached down into the basket, wondering as always how she could possibly squeeze out any more money from her small wage cheque.

Wide-eyed, she read the flamboyant scrawl, and read it through again and then a third time, her face tight and strained, eyes fixed unseeingly on the sun and shadow stippled country ahead.

So! He was coming here! His demands were growing bigger, his ideas more and more ambitious. The fool! What would he say if she suddenly turned on him – throwing aside the cloak of loyalty and sacred vows with which she had ever sought to hide the past, and especially his own despicable conduct?

Ah, tongues would wag as never before and likely Mayor Jenkins would ask for her resignation, if only on account of her young charges. But – it might even be worth it to call Sam's bluff, to cut the ground right under his feet and defy him openly; if necessary answering his accusations with counter-charges! Yet, what of Mike Santeely? His home was right here, in the valley, whatever else!

Slowly she replaced the paper in the envelope, slipping it into the corsage of her dress. There was a wilder light in Dulcie Randell's grey eyes than ever before, as she caught up the reins and set the bay to the last mile stretch...

He was waiting for her as usual, beside the creek, and as Nimrod's buckboard rattled into view along the shallow, piñon-dotted canyon, Mike Santeely stepped from the scrub juniper, lifting his arm in signal to the girl.

54

Less than fifteen minutes later, she was hitching the bay's reins and gazing down at Santeely with a soft, sad warmth in her eyes.

'Dulcie!'

He handed her down from the rig and drew her towards him with impatient gentleness.

'No, Mike – please–'

'What is it, Dulcie? What has happened to change you...?' His hands still gripped her arms but he made no further attempt to embrace her. Instead, his dark gaze searched her face as though in the very expression there, he would find an answer to his question.

'I haven't changed, Mike. Need you ask such a question? Ah, something has happened, yes, and in that you are right! Sam is coming to Latigos! I have only just received his letter–'

'Coming *here*, Dulcie! But why?... Does he figure to–'

This time he released his grip, enabling her to turn back to the rig. 'Maybe he thinks he can get more from me by being on the spot,' she said softly. 'Maybe Mr Sam Fredericks is reckoning on having the same timid, scandal-fearing wife to deal with that he has always had. Wait, Mike! You had best read it for yourself...'

She moved towards him, and as she spoke, retrieved the envelope from her bosom, handing it to Santeely with a soft blush.

Quickly he read the letter and stood staring at the scrawled words long after he had absorbed their full import.

'Come over here, Dulcie, where we can sit and mebbe reason this thing out.' He indicated a spot near the scrub juniper bordering the creek and, after they were seated he drew out papers and tobacco, fingers working mechanically as his mind probed the problem.

'We've got to face up to it, Mike,' Dulcie said after a moment or two. 'It will mean trouble, big trouble!

'If Sam's aiming to live off me and – and even *with* me as he hints, then there will have to be a showdown! Latigos will have to know the truth… Oh, yes. Sam will bring out all the lies with which he has threatened to "expose" me and for which he claims he has "proof"!

'Yes, Mike, if I finally round on him, flinging back his taunts of harlot, scarlet woman–'

'*Dulcie!*'

'Why, Mike. You know at least a few of the things he has said about me. You've seen the letters he has written! Don't be afraid of words – sure, they can harm me, lose me my job perhaps, but so long as the things are not true–'

'But how do you know folks won't believe

him, Dulcie, and throw *you* to the wolves? You know what western communities can be like! Oh, yes, rough, crude, lawless, with their red-light districts! But direct a breath of gossip against a "respectable" citizen and the whole community is up in arms demanding an investigation or worse still mebbe, condemning without a proper hearing!'

'Don't I know all that, Mike! Why, I have been through it a dozen times before. Yet, always, over and above his threats I have always felt–' She shivered involuntarily and turned a wan smile on the man beside her.

'Perhaps it is not loyalty which has held me, but plain cowardice! I guess many women might be excused shrinking from this kind of public attention. Notoriety is maybe a more accurate word to use. All right! So I was scared that if I didn't send him money and more money he would "tell everything" as he put it, even though his "proof", his very thoughts are foul lies–'

'What is this proof that he claims to hold, my dear?' Gently, Santeely laid his hand on Dulcie Randell's arm, shocked that the long simmering volcano had suddenly threatened to erupt, yet stirred at the vital change wrought in this soft-voiced, lovely girl.

'Proof?' she repeated, and laughed softly without humour.

'One example is good enough, I guess, and

likely I should have told you this along with the things before, in all fairness. But you know it was not because I didn't trust you! I – I somehow felt so – so ashamed as well as – afraid! But I'm no longer ashamed or scared. My real worry is not for my own reputation, it is for yours, Mike–'

'Dulcie! D'you imagine I care a row of buttons what folks around here think? Let them put any of those thoughts into words and – so help me God, I'll–'

'I know how you feel, dear, but it isn't always possible to fight gossip, lies, slander. Leastways, they're things you can't fight with your fists or with a gun! This story of Sam's I was about to tell you. It's true really, you see, it's just the – the insinuations, the suggestions in back of it and in back of folks' minds!

'It's true that one night Sam was away from the farm and that a rider came by the same evening. He was a stranger; his horse had stumbled and thrown him.'

Dulcie laid her gaze on the scrub and piñon beyond the creek, on to where the distant blue mountains lifted their white-capped peaks.

'I – I only did what anyone would've done,' she went on, 'or maybe they wouldn't. I don't know–'

'Did he – try to take advantage of you, Dulcie, is that where the trouble lays?'

She laughed bitterly. 'He did at first, yes. Tried to kiss me, asked questions, but I wasn't afraid of him and I think he – he realized and understood. He wasn't a bad man, Mike, just lonely, I guess, and in need of a woman's loving.

'I fixed him a meal. Then he went outside and returned with a whisky bottle from his saddle. I did get a little scared when he started in drinking from the bottle, but after a while he seemed to forget about me. It must've gone on like that for hours, while he drank and smoked, I moved around finding jobs to keep me occupied.

'Finally I had to leave him while I went out to tend the stock and when I got back I found him sprawled across the bed in the next room. He – he was far too big and heavy for me to shift, nor could I wake him from his drunken sleep.' She shrugged as though the whole episode was no longer of any importance.

'I spent a sleepless night on the sofa and somewhere around sunrise fixed some fresh coffee and took him some. He was awake by then, but didn't say anything–'

'Did he ever give you his name or say where he was from?' Mike demanded. 'Because I'm beginning to see what all this is about now, and if we could get hold of him–?'

'I've kicked myself many times since that

night, but generally you don't ask those questions of a guest, not even back in Iowa.'

She loosed the strings under her chin, and removed her bonnet, allowing the breeze and the afternoon sun to touch the dark gold hair.

'He said his first name was Greg. What town or even State he hailed from or where he was bound, I just don't know!

'Well, I figured he would want some breakfast however he was feeling and I went out back to the kitchen and started in on cooking a meal. But when I went through to call him, he was gone! I guess I got panicky then, for some reason, strange though it sounds, and ran outside to the barn looking either for Greg himself or his horse. The next thing I knew, Sam was driving across the yard in the buckboard and he could see right away something had happened.

'There wasn't much I could keep from that – devil, even if I wanted to,' Dulcie continued, 'and inside three-four minutes we were both standing in the bedroom looking at the rumpled quilt – all smeared with bootmarks and dust – and on the floor, an empty whisky bottle!'

'And that swine Sam accused you–'

'I'll never know whether he really believes what his eyes told him or not. Maybe he knows I'm innocent but prefers to think of me as unfaithful. And, as though that was

60

not enough in itself, he found a bill-fold on the bed, empty of money but with the single name "Greg" stamped inside–'

'And ever since,' Santeely gritted, 'he's held this – this purely circumstantial evidence over you–?'

She smiled again, watching the sun's angled rays dapple the high country with splashes of gold. 'It doesn't even have to be evidence when it's a question of ruining a woman's reputation! A whisper here, a glance there – is sufficient. Once she is labelled "harlot", however innocent she may be, she might as well quit right away. Sooner or later she'll have to, which is what I did!'

'It's monstrous, Dulcie! Why are people so – so damnably wicked? Not only Sam Fredericks for dreaming up such an idea but – all the other folk – your friends and neighbours, store-keepers–?'

'I too thought that way at first, Mike. That they were all rotten-bad to – to condemn without–' She broke off, swung her gaze round to Mike's anxious face, seeing the pain and anger in his eyes and of a sudden, feeling a greater surge of love for him than ever before.

Very soberly she leaned over and kissed him on the cheek, a soft, warm yet tender caress, and when he would have drawn her into his arms, she gently held him away.

'Maybe they're not entirely to blame for

acting like they did,' she said quietly. 'The folks back home, I mean. Sam has a way of putting himself over with people and has a fiendish talent for making a situation look bad – not by the things he says but by those he *doesn't* say – leaving it to the imagination so that finally it is others who are spreading stories, doing Sam's dirty work for him whilst he becomes the recipient of sympathy and friendship!'

'Well, you have told me some things about your past, Dulcie, but this beats all hell! Maybe if Fredericks does show up around here, I shall kill him, even if he is your husband!'

'I don't want you to tangle with him, Mike. He can beat most men with his fists and – and I've seen him use a gun! In any case, if it comes to a – a showdown, I may have to move on again, even if Latigos should take my word against his!'

Abruptly she stood up, extending her hand to Santeely. Together they gazed out over the mesas and canyons and the parkland below whereon cattle grazed with unhurried deliberation.

'You have grown up in this country, Mike, and your roots are here. With me it is different; one place is as good as another just so long as communities need someone to teach their children. And thank heavens I can still do that–'

'My roots are plumb liable to be pulled up pretty soon,' he interrupted grimly, 'unless I can think up some smart way of stalling Arrow–'

She swung on him, wide eyes searching his face. 'Arrow? Tell me, Mike! What is it, trouble with Mr Holman?'

He stood silent for a few moments, building a fresh quirly, the girl watching him with a new and growing fear in her heart.

From their very first meeting, seven months back, Dulcie had been drawn to this quiet lonely man, striving to eke out an existence on the homestead section known as the Jarvis strip. And almost without realization, she had at once assessed his weakness and his strength. A harder man than Mike might well have had the good sense to see he was licked and despite long and close associations, pulled stakes and found a new place elsewhere. Not Mike, though. He just struggled on like a punch-drunk fighter, working on with his crops and scrub cattle with a kind of futile determination! Maybe, she thought, that was really the quality she loved best in him.

He spoke now with the controlled outward calm of a man more than halfway resigned to the inevitable yet still doggedly resolved to continue along the chosen trail without deviation.

'Holman's a man with an insatiable

appetite, Dulcie; always hungry for more, whatever he gets! Sure, the Jarvis strip wouldn't make much difference to him, mebbe give him graze enough for up to fifty head is all. But he wants it; even offered me two dollars fifty an acre, coupla weeks back!'

'But – didn't you say you held title deeds that the land had been proved up long ago?'

Santeely nodded. 'Last Monday he sent his foreman, Gil James, with a final offer of three dollars an acre–'

'A *final* offer, Mike? I don't understand!'

'It's quite simple, really. He's willing to pay nine-sixty dollars for the whole section; one thousand, including the cabin.'

'You could do a lot with a thousand dollars, Mike, couldn't you? But what if you–'

'If I refuse? Why, Dulcie,' he said in a low voice. 'That's where the word final comes in. Gil made it clear I could either ride out with a thousand bucks in my jeans, or take the consequences...'

CHAPTER IV

LONELY SHEEP FARM

'Wal, *amigo,* and what do you think of Star-cross?'

Baumann grinned up from the desk. 'Mebbe I should say, "What d'you think of Judith Valdés?"'

'And mebbe I should say what dam' business is it of yours, Will? Come to that, what makes you think I been to Starcross?'

'Are you kiddin'? Likely I don't allus read the sign right, but I reckon this was clear enough. Fust off, you show a deal o' interest when Miss Valdés pulls up in front of Sullivan's – wanta know her name... Next thing, two-three hours later, you're ridin' outa town with Esteban, an' I'd say it ain't stretchin' things too far to conclude you was both headin' fer the Valdés ranch!'

Ventura nodded, moved over to a chair against the wall and sent Baumann a faint smile.

'There's no secret about it anyway,' he admitted. He tipped dry tobacco into a cornpaper, rolling the cylinder between his fingers and thumbs. 'But, strangely, it was

Valdés who invited *me* out there, and not the other way round!'

'How come? Esteban don't usually–'

'Pick up drifting saddle-bums?' Ventura murmured.

The lawman flushed. 'Aw, hell! I didn't say that! Sure, mebbe at fust I was kinda riled. Seemed like everythin' dropped easy fer you, like standin' under a tree and jest waitin' to catch the nearest ripe apple!' Baumann pushed forward from his chair, turned and gazed out through the dusty window onto the thronging boardwalk.

'At the time,' he grunted, 'we was all purty tired an' dispirited. Me an' Kirby'd bin in the saddle better'n thirty hours near continuous. And up around San Pablo, Sheriff Digby an' a half-dozen deppities had bin doin' the same kind of thing.' He laughed shortly.

'We no sooner called it all off when you show up again; the man who pulled in Diamondback Smith, seven-eight months ago!' He drew back from the window and regarded Ventura quizzically.

'Fust time I figgered you was jest plain lucky. But when it happened again, this time with one o' Torch Butler's men, wal, I don't mind admittin' I wasn't the only one as felt a mite suspicious–'

'You mean,' Ventura murmured, 'If I could pull in outlaws like that, then mebbe I was playing some kind of double-cross – even *knew* these men – and every so often, sold one of them down the river?'

'I know it sounds plumb foolish when you put it that way,' Will Baumann acknowledged. 'I reckon Butler would have made it his number one job to get you, was that so!'

Ventura nodded. 'I've never met him, nor any of his partners in crime, savin' Dillis himself, but like I told you, Will, I had a law job once. 'Twas back in California and I learned a few things about bad hats.'

The marshal commenced tamping tobacco into the pipe on his desk. 'Whadda you fixin' to do after Ollie gets back; stick around here or ride on?'

'What's the difference?'

Baumann grunted. 'Mebbe nothing; mebbe a lot!'

'Meaning?'

'You said you was a lawman – once. Reckon though you wouldn't be interested in wearin' a badge agin?'

Ventura smiled and heeled the butt of his cigarette on the floor. 'Sounds mighty close to an invitation for me to stay on, Will. How come? I figgered bounty hunters was considered meaner than the skunks they brought in!'

'All right. You got a reason to feel sore, but a wolf is judged by the pack it runs with, Ventura, an' I ain't tellin' you nothin' you don't know there! I reckon too, you savvy what trouble this breed has caused; frame-ups, double-crosses, even cold-blooded murder with a faked identity, just so's some side-winder kin march up an' claim the reward money! Do you wonder–?'

'I've seen it, too, Marshal. I guess, on balance, I don't blame folk for regarding them as skunks, even though it *could* be an insult to the polecat family in some cases.'

'If you had told me you was–'

But Ventura had moved quickly and silently to the door.

'Hey!' Baumann called. 'Where in Hades you goin'?'

'No place! Just figgered I heard a light wagon turn onto the street...'

Baumann stared at the others in astonishment as he moved to join him at the now open door. 'Sufferin' snakes! Starcross's democrat ain't the only light rig around these parts! Besides which–' the marshal's narrowed gaze sought and found the vehicle downstreet away, part hidden for a moment as a rider crossed in front. '...It ain't what you figgered after all. It's Miss Dulcie comin' back from her Thursday afternoon constitootional, in Hatch Nimrod's buck-board!'

They watched as the sun-bonneted girl steered the bay and rig through the early evening traffic. She had to haul up for a

68

while almost outside the marshal's office as a heavily-laden freight-wagon lumbered slowly out from the intersection ahead.

'Isn't she Miss Randell, the school teacher, Will?'

'Sure is, an' a real nice lady, savin' she seems to spend most of her time alone. Not that there's anythin' wrong in that, I guess–'

'She handles those ribbons well,' Ventura admired, watching the girl rein around the rear of the freight-wagon with inches to spare. 'Reckon she must do a heap of driving?'

Will Baumann nodded, closed the door slowly and returned to his desk.

'Don't think she's ever missed takin' out on a Thursday, since jest after she came here, 'ceptin' in real bad weather. Once-twice she's used a saddler, but most often it's been a rig from the livery stables.'

Ventura built another cigarette, wiped a match alight and then held the flame to the unlit pipe between the marshal's clenched teeth.

'It doesn't seem right somehow.' He blew out the flame and dropped the burnt stick into a heavy china ashtray whilst Baumann waited; stood gazing at the floor for the space of half his cigarette.

'Well, I guess it's none of my business, after all, what Latigos' school teacher does in her spare time–'

'You got somethin' on yore mind, Ventura! What is it that don't seem right to you, fer one thing?'

'Where's Miss Randell supposed to visit when she goes out like this, every Thursday is it?'

'Wal–' Baumann fingered his mournful moustache thoughtfully. 'I don't see anythin' pertikler strange in takin' a regular drive on yore free afternoons, an' her cooped up in a schoolroom all the week. As to where she goes, that ain't no secret, brother. Everyone knows she sometimes drive up to San Pablo, or Plata, where she visits an aunt or somethin'.

'Other times mebbe it's the Griffin homestead across the river. They's a man and his wife an' two kids there. Chel Griffin himself is a right fine saddler, comes into town a coupla times a year an' sells what he's made, loads up with stores, that kinda thing.'

'Sure. But wouldn't you say it was – well, risky, for a pretty girl to sashay around the country on her lonesome, most likely un-armed–?'

'You mean on account of Butler and his gang might still be around here some place?' The marshal frowned. 'I sure didn't like the idea at fust, I'll admit that. Me an' Mayor Jenkins both, was a mite worried in the beginnin', an' I do know Nimrod at the stables is allus warnin' Miss Dulcie to go keerful!

'Wal, I dunno. She jest went right on natcherally drivin' out an' around an' me or Kirby usta ride down the road a way round about five-six o'clock, wait fer her to come along one or other of the trails where they fork an–' Baumann shrugged expressively. 'Guess Miss Dulcie never did cotton to bein' "watched," as she called it. Nothin' ever happened an' we gradually quit the routine of waitin' fer her outside town. Wasn't allus possible, anyway, fer one of us to be there.'

'What other outfits are there in the valley beside Starcross and Arrow?'

Will Baumann looked up in mild surprise. He had to switch his mind abruptly to a subject which seemed on the face of it unrelated to the problem of Miss Randell's weekly drives.

'So you've heard something of Arrow, huh? Wal, take a tip from me an' don't go huntin' trouble *there*. I reckon, Ventura, that yo're a man capable of lookin' out for yore-self. But Mr Holman is big in more ways than one! He's already served on the terri-torial legislature once and likely that won't be the end of it!'

The other nodded. It was not difficult to carry his mind back to last night and re-live the powerful impressions created not only

71

by Judith but, in an entirely different way, by this man Holman. Big, brash, crude and only partially literate, he yet had the ruthless strength of purpose and dominating drive to grasp what many better equipped men might well fail to achieve.

'I guess that means Arrow's a pretty big spread, huh?'

'More'n half the grazin' land in the valley,' Baumann said dryly, 'runnin' mebbe around fifteen-twen'y thousand haid of cattle. Big enough, leastways, fer Gil James, Holman's ramrod to keep a dozen men on the payroll permanent, and hire extra help at round-up.'

'Who else apart from Starcross?'

'Just a small outfit over to the north-west; five-six hundred acres is all, an' run by an old mossyhorn name o' Vic Kaldorp–'

'You figger Holman's fixing to control the entire valley in between shining the seat of his pants at Santa Fe?'

Baumann looked suddenly startled. 'Don't spread that kinda talk around outside, Ventura, not even in fun, else mebbe you'll wind up at bottom of a deep ravine one night!'

'But is he pushing anyone?' Ventura insisted, his mind still on Judith and Esteban Valdés.

The marshal spread his hands. A man was entitled to voice his opinions maybe, except when it came to criticizing or accusing an outfit like Arrow. Power politics were not Will Baumann's line of country, yet he knew well enough that even his own job depended to a very great extent on Roy Holman's say-so. And what of this quiet-spoken, tough Ventura? Was he just a fiddle-foot, riding the grub-line and at other times earning bounty money?

Baumann asked softly. 'What's yore interest in all this, an' what about *you* answerin' *my* questions for a change?'

Ventura smiled. 'That's fair, Will.' He dived one hand into an inner pocket of his brush jacket and came up with a sheriff's star and a crumpled piece of paper. 'At least this'll show you I really was a lawman once! But I'm through with any kind of regular paid law job, Will, an' mebbe some day I'll tell you why.

'I admit I wasn't sure of *you* at first! And don't go off half-cocked! Seems we both had the same idea. Meanwhile, I got the feeling there's something simmering under the lid–'

'You mean here in San Pablo County?'

Ventura nodded, walked slowly up and down the room. 'I got the feeling that quite a few people and quite a few things are mebbe tied together here in the Yerba River valley.' He lifted his shoulders and grinned. 'I guess it's no more than a hunch at the moment, Will. Likely I'm wrong to blazes–'

'You just given me a thought, with what you said,' Baumann broke in. 'I mentioned them three outfits jest now, even Griffin's two-bit place, but I forgot about Mike Santeely fer the moment. Like Griffin, Mike don't come into town much; got a three-twenty acre section called the Jarvis strip, *an' it's kinda sandwiched in the middle of Arrow*—'

'Tell me, Will,' Ventura said softly...

Charlie Williams stood staring after Esteban as horse and rider disappeared in the slowly rising mists of early dawn. 'I want the roan saddled, Charlie,' was what Valdés had said and this was the third or fourth time during recent months that the *jefe* had insisted on riding the most nondescript-looking animal from the Starcross string. Moreover, it was the only horse which Esteban refused to have branded with the Starcross mark. It carried a faint, almost indecipherable S.O. on its rump and as far as Charlie or Glen Summers knew, the initials didn't mean a dam' thing!

Williams turned his head at the sound of boots crunching on gravel. The *segundo* was walking towards him from the bunkhouse, tasting his first cigarette in the sharp, scent-filled dawn air.

'What's up, Charlie? You look kinda worried.' Glen Summers, like the roan gelding, only in a different way, was also rather

74

nondescript in appearance. He had the face and unobtrusive characteristics of a man difficult to catalogue. Folk rarely remembered what he looked like after meeting him. Maybe it was because his features were regular with no particular accentuation on eyes, nose or mouth. His sparse hair and moustache were a mouse-brown, and in a crowd he could stand quietly unobserved, unnoticed so that afterwards it was difficult to be sure that he had been present at all. Nevertheless, in his quiet way, Glen Summers was a good stockman; knew cattle, and, on the face of it at least, managed the outfit well enough, and with the four other hands generally executed Esteban's instructions intelligently.

Charlie shoved back his hat and scratched.

'Cain't understand why he wants to ride that crow-bait sometimes, Glen, an' when he does–' The oldster shut his mouth abruptly, conscious suddenly of a feeling of guilt. Even discussing Esteban's odd behaviour with Summers seemed kind of mean. Unthinkingly he had spoken his mind and had communicated part of his puzzled concern to a man for whom he normally had little time.

'What are you tryin' to say, Charlie; what's all this about the boss ridin' crow-bait–?'

A sly look crept into the oldster's blue eyes but when he turned to Summers, his glance held only a bland innocence.

'Why, nothin' really, Glen. Jest that whenever Esteban rides out to see a cattle-buyer, he picks about the doggonedest piece o' hoss-flesh... Don't even bother with wearin' his best suit neither!'

Williams laughed easily. 'Mebbe he's smart at that and figgers he kin beat the guy down a few bucks per haid–'

'He didn't tell me he was seein' any cattle-buyer!' Summers' voice was low-pitched and flat as usual, yet the wrangler detected a faintly metallic ring underneath and knew Glen was either inwardly angry or else – mebbe suspicious!

He grinned amicably at the *segundo*. 'Y'know how he is sometimes, Glen – kinda moody. Why, he only mentioned it to me by accident I reckon. Even now he ain't figgerin' on doin' any real buyin' this trip. Said somethin' about takin' a looksee at some hombre's shorthorn herd.'

'And he didn't say where – or who this feller was?'

'Naw! Only found out *that* much in time it took me t'saddle up a hoss.' Williams sidled up to the Starcross *segundo*, and gave the man a meaningful look. 'Way I see it, Glen, Valdés ain't got the *dinero* to go buying' much new stock!'

'Just the way I had it figgered, Charlie,' Summers muttered and walked slowly back towards the bunkhouse.

Charlie Williams' mind returned to the early spring morning when Summers and two of the boys, Lace Tortville and Ed Colfax had ridden back with the fateful news! All the three hundred-odd head of sleek cattle, gathered for the trail drive to Fort Frazer, had been found dead and dying on a section of the range broken and crossed with dry washes. There was no locoweed growing on Starcross; leastways none that could be reached by cattle. This had been hauled in and fed to the herd during the night.

Charlie remembered too, that the new boys, Jack and Red Fletcher, had been given the chore of night-hawking the trail herd. Considering they had only been on the payroll a couple of weeks, this was unusual at least. But herding the stock and apportioning work to the riders was Summers' job and unlikely even Esteban would have queried the *segundo's* judgment.

Sure, Glen had taken full responsibility, said it was his fault for trusting the two new hands, even offered to quit there and then, but the Valdés wouldn't hear of it. They just went on as though nothing had happened, keeping the misery back behind a steady smile.

But, all along, Charlie Williams had felt sure the vanished Fletcher brothers had not done this thing on their own. They had been *paid* for that diabolical crime and it stood to reason, whoever planted them there at Starcross, was someone anxious to give the Valdés the final shove which would land them over the brink to complete ruin. How Miss Judith and Esteban had gotten through the last couple of months, the oldster didn't quite know. But he knew that the quiet spoken, hard-working Glen had hired the Fletcher boys, claiming that the extra wages would be more than covered by the time factor. It might mean Starcross getting their dinero from the beef contract three four weeks earlier than expected. But there had been no dinero because there had been no herd. What remained on Starcross grass was mostly older beef steers and a couple of hundred cow critturs who had yet to drop their this year's calves. Right along Holman had been Charlie's sure choice and now, as he watched the *segundo* disappear into the bunkhouse, he became suddenly convinced that Glen Summers was the tool which Holman had used...

Beyond sight of the home buildings, Esteban reined his mount from the dirt road and took off at a gentle lope across country. Every so often, he veered and doubled back; twice he put the roan to a creek, but instead of crossing, he rode for a distance over the rock and gravel bottom before finally climbing the shallow bank opposite.

By such a series of twists and turns and water crossings, he left sign such as even might fool an Apache, and yet contrived to push steadily south-westward, away from the grassy rangeland mesas and benches and on into a smooth stretch of sheep-farming land almost entirely enclosed by bluffs on the south and east and by thickly wooded slopes to the west.

Valdés continued unerringly through a volcanic fissure in the bluffs, emerging quite suddenly into a meadow of cropped grass. Ahead, no more than a quarter mile lay the farmhouse, single-storied, stone-built with a wooded shingle roof. A short distance away from the house and outbuildings, a man reclined in the forenoon sun, hat tilted well forward over his eyes.

Valdés rode on along the single track leading to the fenced yard and reined to a halt about a dozen paces from the recumbent guard.

'You want some woollies, mister?'

Esteban held his hands in full view and smiled thinly. 'It's the golden fleece I'm interested in!'

The guard rose to his feet without taking his gaze off the new-comer. 'Who's callin', mister?'

'Steve Crow's the name; here to see Mr Butler!'

The man grinned. 'Steve Crow, huh! Guess you ain't bin on many shearin' jobs have you?'

'No. Plata was the first.'

'Wal, Crow, let's hope it won't be the last.' He laughed softly and for a fearful moment Esteban thought something had gone wrong! But the guard made no move to draw the gun at his hip. Instead he jerked his head towards the house and stepped back a pace. 'It's okay, mister. You can go up–'

'*Gracias, amigo,*' Valdés said and was careful to use the Border accent.

He gigged the tired roan over to a rack, unshipped and hitched the reins. A big, chunky-looking man in a broadcloth coat and striped trousers, stood in the open doorway. His putty-coloured face appeared even more sallow by contrast with the dark greasy hair and fiercely waxed moustache.

He grinned wolfishly, black eyes darting every which-way. 'Light down an' rest, Crow,' he invited in a thick voice. He motioned Esteban to follow, and led the way into the same small room as before.

'Seddown, Crow.' He indicated a shabby overstuffed chair across from the desk and Valdés seated himself, cuffing back his dust-powdered hat with a careless, impatient gesture; a typical *Americano* flourish, this, and one of many which he had so carefully and secretly rehearsed.

'Everythin' go all right, Mr Butler?' Esteban's quiet drawl, his air of latent toughness – these things had influenced Torch Butler from the very beginning.

He grinned again and nodded his big head. 'Sure it did, Crow, an' you did what you was told – just like the other boys–' An inner door opened and Butler glanced up sharply. The new-comer, almost a replica of Torch himself, stepped into the room.

'Guess you didn't meet my brother before, he was away at the time! Jim! This is Steve Crow – come to collect on the Plata job.'

Jim Butler nodded briefly, eased one hip on to the desk and withdrew a cigar from his pocket. Esteban caught a flash of the shell-belt and two guns as the man's frock-coat swung open.

'Here's the list,' Torch said, pushing a sheet of paper across the desk for Valdés to glance at. 'Everythin' all square an' above board y'see,' he grinned. 'We lifted twen'y-two thousand dollars countin' notes, coin and dust. You know the rules, Crow. Your cut is five per cent, like we agreed. That's eleven hun'ed dollars; less one hundred for outa-pocket expenses, leaves you a clear thousand. Satisfied?'

'Sure.'

Valdés fished for his Durham sack, rolled and lit a quirly with detached interest. *Think much but talk little,* was what Judith would say!

'Reckon we wasn't too sure of you at first, Steve,' the outlaw went on, 'but Jim here was watchin' you even though you didn't know it!'

Valdés shivered inwardly and glanced up with a cold smile. He reached for the gold poke which Butler had pushed towards him, casually stuffed it inside his buckskin shirt.

'Mebbe it would be better to watch the hombres who was slingin' lead at us, 'stead o' watchin' each other,' he drawled, and held his breath while a sticky silence spread throughout the room like an ever widening pool of molasses.

Jim Butler put a sulphur match to his cigar and puffed clouds of blue smoke before laying the spent match in a bowl.

'We welcome suggestions, Crow – helpful ones! But we don't take kindly to criticisms like that. If Torch an' me wasn't mighty careful who we took in – well, we wouldn't be operatin' for long now, would we?'

'He's right, Steve.' Torch smiled. 'You jest let *us* do the thinkin' an' we'll get along fine–'

''Stá bueno.' Valdés got to his feet. 'I could use some more of this kind of dinero! You got anythin' else lined up–'

Butler nodded. 'Seddown an' I'll tell you, but we still got to hear from Dillis, our look-out man in the San Pablo area–'

'I was comin' to that,' Esteban said, 'an' I reckon you won't be hearing from Hank Dillis in a long time!'

Their hard gazes fastened on to Esteban's face. 'What exactly do you mean?' Jim Butler asked softly.

'I reckon then, you couldn't 've heard that a bounty hunter called Ventura picked up Dillis and took him into Latigos...'

CHAPTER V

DEATH SMILES FOR GIL JAMES

'You mean,' Torch Butler asked slowly, 'Hank Dillis has bin arrested; is in the jail there at Latigos right now?'

'More than that – in a way,' Valdés replied, 'for he was escorted to the county seat almost at once. Reckon he's in care of Sheriff Digby...'

'How d'you know all this, Crow?' Jim Butler knocked ash from the tip of his cigar, eyes lifting again to Valdés. 'And who's this Ventura? A bounty hunter, you say! How d'you know he ain't an undercover lawman–?'

Esteban shook his head. 'I'm pretty sure

he's just what he claims to be – a fiddle-foot after any reward money he can pick up–'

'Dillis ain't no easy meat,' Torch growled, 'he's smart and he's fast with a gun!'

Valdés shook his head. 'I've not seen this Ventura hombre in action, but he looks tough enough–'

'You sure it was Ventura got onto Dillis and not the law?'

'I met him in Latigos the day after,' Valdés said carefully. 'The whole town was buzzin', figured mebbe you had heard–'

'He was our only man in that district,' Jim Butler said. 'We've bin expectin' him to ride in any day now.'

'Is he going to talk?' Esteban's softly-voiced question at once focused attention on the possibilities of their personal plight.

Torch said: 'Dillis won't talk. For one thing, he knows the Butler brothers look after their men!'

'What does that mean?'

'It means,' Jim replied, 'that as soon as we've checked he's at San Pablo for trial, we'll – get him away!'

'Supposin' that's just not possible?' Valdés persisted.

'Why,' Torch smiled, 'when he comes outa the pen, we'll have a nice sum of money waitin' for him. It's one of the rules a man's five per cent is credited against his name all the while he's up country!'

'This might make a difference to the next job, Torch.' Jim Butler laid his smoke down, crossed over to the door and opened it. 'Louis!' he called, 'rustle up some coffee an' sandwiches!' He closed the door again and returned to his perch on the desk.

'Ventura,' he muttered, 'that name sounds kinda familiar! Now, where–?'

Valdés smiled grimly. 'Just what I thought when I heard it! Then I remembered that nearly a year back a man picked up five hundred dollars' reward money on account of taking Diamondback Smith, one of Ketchum's members. The hombre's name was Ventura!'

'Seems to me,' Torch said turning to his brother, 'Steve here'd be mighty useful actin' as undercover look-out man, 'specially while Hank is – away!'

The other nodded thoughtfully. 'What else, Crow? You didn't get around to finding out how much this Ventura bustard knows, did you?'

'I even talked to him.' Esteban shrugged slightly. 'You wouldn't expect a man like that to tell the story in detail. But three things stick out, the way I have it figured. First, the fellow must've stumbled across something which led him to Dillis. Second, the way he wears his gun I'd say he was likely pretty handy at slinging it. Third, just a blind hunch that he's also a dam' good trailer–'

85

'He needs takin' care of,' Torch said. 'If yore figgerin's right, Steve, an' mebbe it is, this guy sounds too dangerous to have around!'

Again Valdés weighed his chances carefully. Yet when he spoke, his words carried the weight of sound reasoning; his reaction a natural enough one to the Butler brothers.

'Count me out on that,' he smiled. 'Like I said, I talked with this hombre an' likely folk'd remember that, 'specially the Marshal of Latigos. If you plan any kind of – accident, betta give me the chance to establish a cast-iron alibi first. The more I can steer clear of men like Sheriff Digby an' Marshal Baumann, the more use I can be to you–'

'That sure makes sense, Jim!' Torch Butler exclaimed. 'I–' A knock broke into the gang leader's words and Louis entered carrying a tray with a pile of roughly cut sandwiches, coffee pot and cups. He set them down on a small table, nodded to the room in general and withdrew.

'Help yourself, Steve,' Torch invited, grabbing himself some of the food. Jim Butler moved over and poured the thick java into the cups.

'You done a good job, bringin' this information,' Torch mumbled through the mouthful of food. 'Reckon this time we'll forget about the "expenses".' He pushed five gold pieces across the desk and Valdés dropped the coins into his pants' pocket with a murmured *'gracias.'*

Nearly an hour later, astride a fresh horse, Esteban headed out from the Butlers' isolated sheep farm. Away to his left he could hear the worried-sounding bleating of sheep. Once he glimpsed a rider, aided by a dog, hazing a flock into an enclosed pasture.

He rode slowly at first, giving full attention to his back trail: not so much in an attempt to confuse the sign as to assure himself he was not being followed. It was quite on the cards that the outlaw brothers might have had him trailed. They still didn't know as much about him as they would have liked. That much was obvious by the further questions asked both directly and obliquely. Where exactly did he live? In Latigos itself, or some other place in the Yerba valley? Was he known to many people? What calling did he follow, or pretend to? Had he any relatives and – one of the insistent questions – was there a woman with whom he might be especially friendly...?

Five-six miles from the Butler hideout, Esteban reined his horse to one side of the winding game trail and considered every aspect of a set-up in which he self-admittedly figured as the Judas of the piece!

He could not shake off the feeling of self-contempt and loathing, even though a hundred times he had argued there was no other way; no honourable alternative at least. But where was the honour in consorting with thieves and murderers? Stealing money from the bank at Plata! Maybe on this next job it would be money belonging to the people of San Pablo or his friends in Latigos itself! Maybe, next time it wouldn't end with a few hurriedly placed shots – someone would get killed! Already now Ventura was a marked man and for him, Esteban's one-time guest at the *casa,* the sands had commenced to run out!

He wiped sweat from his face and fashioned a quirly, searching for consolation in the realization that whatever it cost, Judith might not now have to contract herself in marriage with a man such as Holman.

This thousand dollars would pay a few of the more pressing debts, maybe give them time to build up; to save the Valdés' land, the Valdés' name– He caught himself up on that thought, conscious that there would be no name to save, if ever he were taken, or identified as Esteban José Cuervo y Valdés! Perhaps, too, it had been foolhardy to assume a *seudónimo* which was the American counterpart of his own! But whatever had been said or done was so much water down the river. He had to start in memorizing those details of the next raid with which

Torch Butler had supplied him. It would also be necessary to figure out some plausible tale for Judith...

Will Baumann had said the stage from San Pablo was due in at six. Likely enough Ollie Kirby would be aboard, carrying a black satchel containing two hundred dollars. Yet, instead of strolling down along towards the stage office, Ventura made his way with long reaching strides to the livery.

Hatch Nimrod was rubbing down a travel-stained bay, and Ventura recognized it as the same animal that had been harnessed to the buckboard Dulcie Randell had driven earlier on. The rig, he now saw, was over to one side of the runway, wheels and body-work layered with trail-dust.

'Looks like Miss Randell sure enjoys driving around,' Ventura smiled. 'Saw her on Main just a while back and she was handling that rig like a ranch hand!'

Nimrod straightened up from his task and nodded. The fact that this Ventura was not unappreciative of such things pleased the liveryman. What if he were a bounty hunter? So far, he'd surely done good in turning that Dillis over to the law, and besides which – Esteban Valdés had seen fit to invite him out to Starcross yesterday, so the talk ran.

'I guess yo're right, Mr Ventura, but I ain't at all sure it's wise fer a purty woman like that to go drivin' around the country on her lonesome.'

'Mebbe you're right, but the marshal was telling me she visits an aunt in Plata?'

'Sure, sometimes. But today f'r instance she wanted to do some quiet readin' so she heads out along the river. Musta gone quite some distance judgin' by the bay here!

'Wal, I guess I'd better get on,' the oldster grinned, reaching for curry comb and brush. 'Was you wantin' the steel-dust saddled?'

'You carry on, Hatch,' Ventura said and walked over to the stall where the horse was tied. A few minutes later, he rode from the livery stables, turned onto Main and headed north, shortly leaving the town behind him.

The sun had perhaps two hours to go before it would drop from sight beyond the San Mateo range and Ventura intended making the best use of the day's remaining light. He could see the faint lines made by the buckboard despite the breeze that shifted the surface dust. And, even though he was half-expecting the tracks to deviate, he was mildly surprised when they swung off suddenly from the road and onto a wide grass verge.

For Ventura, it was almost as clear following sign across country, as over a defined trail or road; sometimes, in a way, even easier. Though the buckboard was light,

90

especially with only a woman aboard, the sign was fresher than a new-laid egg; barely a few hours old. Moreover, Miss Randell had used the same route on her homeward journey as the outward one. Where one set of tracks grew faint, petered away, the other was often more clearly visible.

Only twice did he have to dismount and cast around before again cutting sign. Mostly, it was plain enough; the pressed down grass not yet fully sprung back; broken twigs and fallen leaves where the wheels had whipped at some trailing vine or shrub; fresh scratches on the rockier ground as a wheel or an iron shoe had struck with a sharper than normal violence.

Thus, in a series of gradual ascents, sometimes over red sandstone and shale, frequently across tawny mesa grass, the tracks made by horse and rig sign-posted a way for Ventura clear through a shallow piñon-fringed canyon and onwards to a grass expanse; to the right, scrub juniper and scrub oak gave indication of the creek beyond.

Not for the first time since he had impulsively set out did Ventura ask himself exactly what he expected or hoped to discover. Probably nothing beyond the fact that for some reason best known to herself, Miss Dulcie Randell had lied about her trip this afternoon! Nimrod had innocently volunteered the information that she had

91

intended driving along the bottom lands of the Yerba. Quite certainly she had been up here and, Ventura saw at once, *had rendezvoused with someone at this very spot!*

Thoughtfully he dismounted, ground anchored the gelding and spent the last remaining moments of full daylight in a careful scrutiny of the scuffed grass and earth hereabouts...

Shortly, with the sun now dipping behind the western mountain range, he built a smoke and pondered on his discoveries for what they were worth. He recalled what Will Baumann had told him about Dulcie during those last few minutes in the marshal's office there. Everyone in Latigos knew the school teacher was, in fact, married, living apart from her husband and using her birth name in preference to the married one of Mrs Samuel Fredericks. There was no 'funny business' about Miss Randell, according to Latigos, because right from the first she had made these things clear, even to the continued wearing of her wedding ring!

But today at least, maybe other times, she had driven up here for a secret meeting with someone! Sure, maybe there was an innocent enough explanation but whatever it was, the sign spread around had its own story to tell!

Ventura had found where a saddle horse

had been tethered and indentations in the grass showed that the buckboard had stood for some time.

He looked out over the misting benchland, studying the landmarks; the tree-lined river partly visible at one point; the distant blue mountains to the north and to the west. He was searching his memory for details of the scant information he had acquired concerning this country and as dusk darkened into night, he grinned slowly, realizing at last that likely enough this place was the Jarvis strip, or near to it; the section Baumann had described as sandwiched in between the higher sweeps of Arrow rangeland. So! Not too far away from here in one direction or another, would be Mike Santeely's cabin. Was it stretching things too far then, to assume that Miss Randell's tryst had been with Santeely? Well, supposing it were true and where in hell was all this getting him beyond the satisfying of an idle curiosity?

Yet he knew well enough he had not come here for the ride alone or entirely to fulfil a sudden whim. Maybe at the back of his mind had been a nebulous, scarcely formed idea that Miss Randell's little secret might be tied in with other mysterious doings in the Yerba valley!

Esteban Valdés, for example, was a cool one and had seemed uncommonly interested in the story of Hank Dillis. What of the lovely Judith and the crude domineering Roy Holman? Where did these people fit in and were the threads of their lives inextricably woven together for obvious reasons or because of deep and sinister motives?

The stars were bright now in a clear, darkening sky, and Ventura scowled and struck the saddle horn with his balled fist, recalling again Holman's brash talk last night and the manner in which his bold, black gaze had crawled over Judith Valdés. Of a sudden, he caught up the steel-dust's reins, hauling himself into leather and gently rowelling his mount forward to skyline.

From this point of vantage, he gazed down over the black silhouettes of brush and piñon, searching the night shadows for any chance glimmering of light. It was a hundred to one against, he told himself. Even if Santeely's cabin were within a two-three mile radius, it was scarcely feasible to expect– He was all set to neck-rein the gelding when his glance caught the merest streak of bright chrome away over to the north-west.

By sheer luck, he had hit the narrow trail which Santeely himself used to approach this plateau creek, but Ventura had to feel his way in the darkness, with only the stars as yet to brighten his way. There were occasional dry arroyos on either side of the twisting ribbon trail, dangerous enough at night time to spell disaster. Mostly, he left it to the steel-dust's instinctive sure-footedness and in a little while the path levelled and broadened out onto a wide clearing.

Less than a quarter-mile away, the cabin showed up vague and dark against its background of brush and scattered trees and Ventura was able to pin-point the half-draped window through which the shaft of light still carried.

He remained still and quiet in the saddle, absorbing the small sounds of the night whilst his narrowed gaze probed ahead, all at once intercepting a second shaft of light, this time showing dully from the further side of the house. It looked, he thought, as though it might be coming from a half-open door.

Why was he acting in this over-cautious way? he wondered, approaching, with all the quiet circumspection of a hunter stalking its 'prey'! This was not Hank Dillis' place to be studied so warily. True, Mike Santeely did not expect him; likely enough would not even identify the name. Added to this was the usual hazard of coming up on a lone man's place at night!

Yet there was something curbing Ventura, and, accordingly he gave instinct its rein and almost at once heard the muted scuffle; the soft jingle of bridle chain. He leaned forward, placing firm gentle fingers on the steel-dust's muzzle and waited out the space of several minutes before unshipping and trying the gelding to a stout brush stem.

Silently, Ventura approached the deep shadows of a juniper stand, knowing himself for a fool to chance his life for no good reason. Why does a man do such things? *Quién sabe?* And even at that moment, he could find a dry humour through his own foolhardiness and laughed silently, for who was there to mourn him?

He moved like a shadow amongst shadows and saw the tethered horse as no more than a black, slow-moving shape; hooves clumping on the soft grass as the animal sought graze within the confines of its tied reins.

Even when he approached near, the pony gave no shrill nicker as Ventura might have expected, but twitched its ears and tail and winked an eye as it took the sugar lumps from his outstretched hand.

It was almost too dark in here to read the brand even close up. But it was newly burned into the short-clipped, silken coat and Ventura's finger traced an A and a five inch lazy rail below. Lazy Rail? No! This was Arrow...!

He was away as quietly as he had come, and clear of the juniper grove, he sped towards the cabin, reaching the unfenced yard as a man's voice sounded through the night. Though the words were softly spoken, they slammed into Ventura's brain with the impact of a bullet from a gun.

'So it's going to be a cold-blooded killing after all, James! What about Holman's offer and what makes him or you figger you can get away with murder? There's a law of sorts–'

The other man's voice was low-pitched with the deadly aridness of the desert, as though its owner had long since been wrung dry of all emotion.

'I told yuh, Mike, Mr Holman changed his mind. I guess he figgered yuh was too ornery to sell anyways! Ain't that the truth now, Mike? Do tell!'

From behind the angled door, Ventura both saw and heard.

The man with his hands tied behind his back was Santeely, of course. A slim, medium built hombre, with an almost scholarly face; not above thirty-five years and handsome enough for Dulcie Randell to find an appeal there, Ventura thought, perhaps something more.

'Mebbeso, James!' Santeely's voice was hoarse with a dry-mouthed fear. He was fighting desperately hard not to break; not to reveal the streak which he knew only too well existed inside him. 'Mebbe I'm just not the kind to let others walk over me,' he said.

'Not even the Holmans or the Gil Jameses of this world–'

'Why, you–'

'Sure! You can best me with yore fists, James, and shoot faster and straighter than ever I could, but I'm still fightin' you, even though mebbe you don't know it. An' I'm still fightin' Holman. He won't be through with me even when you've killed me! I'll–'

'Yuh sure are crazy, Santeely, now ain't yuh?'

The other shook his head. The dank hair flopped across his forehead. Even from the patch of shadow in which he stood by the door, Ventura marked the pallid face, the trickle of sweat, the instinctive moistening of over dry lips. Santeely knew he was facing death and whatever his fears and his weaknesses, he still wouldn't *crawl* to this Arrow gun-fighter! Ventura felt a swift surge of admiration for this lone nester who had no weapons save his own dogged defiance. Nor could the bounty hunter but wonder for a brief moment at the strange chance that had brought him here; starting as it had as no more than a mild curiosity regarding Dulcie Randell and finishing in a sudden-born resolve to find and talk with the Jarvis Strip homesteader.

'By God!' Santeely choked. 'Why don't you get it over with – what you waitin' for? There's nothin' else to say – except one thing, mebbe–'

'Spit it out, Mike. But if it's jest cuss words yuh kin save yuhr breath!' His glance moved over Santeely with a studied unconcern, but for Ventura the whole, quietly-enacted scene held the macabre quality of an evil nightmare.

'Why – why is Holman – doin' this – just for a few acres of scrub and grass–?'

'Yuh ought've figgered that one out, Santeely, knowin' what you do about Mr Holman!'

'You – mean – because I accidentally witnessed the killing of those Starcross men?'

'Sure. Them Fletcher kids got a mite uppish after doctorin' Starcross's trail-herd, an' Mr Holman don't stand for blackmail, Mike–'

'But – I never did anything about it! I could've gone to San Pablo and sworn a statement – demanded protection–'

'That ain't to say yuh mightn't still do it,' James pointed out. 'An' with Mr Holman runnin' for the Santa Fe legislature–' he shrugged. The answer was so simple it needed no further elaboration.

'There's – somethin' else!' Santeely cried in desperation; but the Arrow ramrod shook his head. 'Ain't got any more time to waste now, Mike–'

'Hold it!'

In one stride Ventura was across the

99

threshold and into the room, legs spread wide, hard gaze boring into James, and each man's right hand was spread like claws over the butt of his holstered gun. And still no sign of emotion abraded the surface of Gil James' swart, bearded face; only the merest flicker of surprise stirred in the deep-set, pale eyes.

'Who in hell are yuh, hombre?' The thin lips scarcely moved. 'Yuh're Gawdamighty lucky I never drew—'

'Now's your chance, James! *I'm callin' you....*'

Maybe for the space of a long drawn out breath, no movement and no sound ruffled the still silence. At some split-second point in that desperate, death-charged moment, Gil James knew for the first time in his life he faced possible death at the hands of a gunman at least his equal. Then and then only did the dark face tighten and the washed-out eyes scintillate like pale azure stones.

His hand closed, flashed up, six-gun clear of leather and hammer drawn back in the winking of an eye.

But Ventura too had drawn with blurring speed, and the long, blue barrelled Colt's gun leaped into his hand like a live thing, breathing flame. Two explosions rocked and echoed within the four walls of Mike Santeely's cabin and between those staccatoed shots lay a period of time too small to measure.

Ventura felt the whip of the bullet's passage as it screamed past, scorching the bandana at his neck and sweat glistened his face as he tore back the gun hammer for a second shot.

But James had taken the first bullet full in the chest, close enough in to the heart for Death to smile and reach out a beckoning finger.

If any expression swam for a second in James' glazing eyes, it was again no more than a cold ripple of surprise. He tried fighting back, but the hour-glass stood empty and the pistol slid from his fingers and crashed to the floor. A moment or two and Gil James fell in a crumpled heap beside his smoking gun.

Ventura pulled his gaze away and stepped across to the white-faced Santeely. With three strokes of his knife, he slashed through the rawhide bonds at Mike's wrists. He said in a thick, croaking voice: 'If you've got a bottle of whisky hereabouts, Santeely, now is the time to open it, by God...!'

CHAPTER VI

THREE HORSES – TWO RIDERS

Esteban brought the jaded horse into the yard and climbed stiffly from the saddle. He stood spraddle-legged a moment, too weary for movement.

Charlie eyed both horse and rider in frank bewilderment. This was no way to return from the routine chore of meeting a cattle-buyer; drunk-weary, dust-covered and with a jaded sweat-streaked horse.

He looked again at the animal and swore under his breath. It was an ugly, nondescript roan all right, sufficiently like the one Esteban had ridden this morning to fool most anyone. And there was the same faint S.O. mark on the rump! Yet, the wrangler was prepared to swear it wasn't the same animal, and he would dam' soon know for sure when it came to grooming. But what the hell! He would get no satisfaction from the *jefe* even should he ask, and in Esteban's present uncertain mood, maybe he would tell him to mind his own dam' business!

'Good trip?' Charlie asked, catching up the reins, and was surprised when Valdés turned a smile on him and nodded, seemingly affable despite obvious fatigue.

'I had to travel out beyond San Pablo,' he explained. 'But it was worth it, Charlie, to see those pure-bred shorthorns! Some of the finest English cattle ever shipped over here–'

'You buy some then?'

'No-o, not yet. But I've acquired an option on enough to form the nucleus of the finest pedigree herd this territory has seen.'

He grinned widely, teeth a flare of white against the dark, dust-caked face, and turned to walk slowly towards the house as Judith appeared on the *pavimento.*

'Heavens, Esteban! I have been worried! Charlie and Glen said something about your meeting a cattle buyer, but you didn't tell me. And you've been gone so long. Nearly all day. What is all the mystery...?'

'Will you quit for a moment, *chiquita,* and let me get inside?' he smiled. Somehow when Esteban allowed himself to smile his face underwent a complete transformation. Good looking as he was, a sullen cloud so often shrouded his brow. But now, despite his physical condition, the cloud was gone, and Judith felt a thrilling lightness of heart as she caught her brother's arm, half dragging him now into the welcome coolness of the flagged interior.

'Give me a half-hour, Jude, and open a

103

bottle of tequila while you're waiting.'

She touched his arm, eyes half-smiling, half-mystified. 'What is it, Steve – you sound – you look almost as though you have good news–?'

'I have,' he grinned, and took the stairs two at a time, weariness temporarily forgotten.

Some twenty minutes later, he joined Judith in the living room, glancing appreciatively at the array of cold meats and spiced foods on the tray.

'You are hungry, Steve. Perhaps you would like to eat right away–?'

'A drink first, *chiquita.*' He reached for the glass of wine which she had poured, and surveyed her quizzically. 'You don't often call me Steve, now, do you?'

'Well, how often do you call me *chiquita?* I – I don't understand you tonight. You seem – oh, I don't know – different somehow–'

'I *feel* different, Jude,' he smiled, seating himself at the table, 'and so will you when you see this–' He withdrew a leathern poke from the pocket of his coat and poured the contents onto the table before her.

'Feast your eyes on it, *chiquita.* You have a perfect right to do so, for it is mine – ours – and, likely there will be more to come – later.'

Wide-eyed, Judith stared unbelievingly at the shining heap of gold and silver pieces before transferring her gaze back to Esteban. Despite the fact he was smiling, she observed a tautness in his face, in his whole manner. Yet there was far too much excitement in her right now to examine such elusive impressions. Natural enough, that Steve should be dog-tired having been away all day. And whatever this deal he had pulled off, likely enough it had not been easy.

'Eleven hundred dollars there,' he told her; 'enough mebbe for us to keep going–'

'How did you get it, Steve? We've nothing left to sell–'

'Oh yes we have, *chiquita!* Something right here under our very noses. Grazing rights! This money represents a year's advance payment for the lease of Starcross grass and water...'

'You mean you've *sold out*–?'

'I said *leased*, didn't I, Jude! Why don't you keep quiet and hear the whole story?' A rising note of irritation crept into his voice. At one gulp he finished his drink, crossed over to the *cajoneria* and refilled the glass with the fiery tequila.

'Don't you think you ought to eat something?' Judith's voice was softly soothing but her straight dark brows drew together as she looked again towards the table.

'Sure, I'll eat, just as soon as I've told you everything!' There was a faint swagger to his walk as he came back across the room.

'I haven't sold anything belonging to you – or me, for that matter. All it means is that a certain rancher I met, wants to use our graze for his herd. I saw some of the stuff, Jude, prime pedigree stock from England. Maybe we'll have enough dinero presently to buy some; start up a shorthorn bunch of our own.

'Meanwhile, we–'

'But, Steve! Eleven hundred dollars for a year's lease – for all this land–?'

'I'm coming to that, *chiquita,* if you will give me the chance.' He ran his hand over the glittering pyramid of coins. 'Not a fortune or anything near, but enough to square our credit in town – mebbe more. But don't you see, Judith, we've got grass to spare, acres of it, and this herd will not interfere with Starcross stock. Only thing is that Glen and the boys will have to nurse them and hold the young stuff along with their mothers–'

'But we shall have to brand them, surely; use this rancher's mark whatever it is?'

'Sure.' Esteban waved his arm in a vague gesture. 'But we haven't fixed those details yet. Why, I don't even know when this hombre–'

'What did you say the rancher's name is?'

'I didn't! But he's some stock-breeder from Colorado, name of Latimer, I think – George Latimer. I'll be seeing him again soon, mebbe in a week or so and fix things. Why, Jude, you don't seem as pleased as I figured you would be. You don't think I–?'

She came over, placing her hands one on each side of her brother's face and tilting his head gently upwards to look deep into his eyes.

'I don't think anything, Steve, except that you're wonderful to have thought of this and actually – pulled it off. It – it has all come as such a surprise, I guess I feel more confused than anything else, except pleased and grateful–'

'What's troubling you, Judith?' It was Valdés' turn now to search.

All day, until this moment, his mind and being had been wholly occupied with the part he had to play; his thoughts centred to the exclusion of almost everything else on Torch Butler, the money, plans for the next job, and perhaps above all else the exercising of such extreme caution and character-acting as would guarantee the continued existence of Steve Crow as well as that of Esteban José Cuervo y Valdés.

The one thing which he had doubted more than anything else had been his ability to put over a story sufficiently convincing enough to satisfy Judith. And, in doing this, he had watched and listened only for certain reactions, rejecting all else as being incidental. But suddenly, with the distasteful

107

chore of lying accomplished, he knew that something else occupied her; a problem perhaps not even concerned with the pressing weight of their financial worries.

'What makes you ask such a question, Steve? There's nothing troubling me beyond the normal–'

He stood up and caught her by the shoulders, concerned and yet relieved that her mind was no longer entirely on his news. There were few things that these two people could hide from each other and Esteban cast around in his mind as he studied Judith's pale face, her lovely eyes now half-veiled to hide what might lie in their depths.

'Is it Holman, Jude? Is it that you don't want to marry him? Ah, but I know he is crude, uneducated, a self-made man whose god is wealth and power and whose skin is tougher than the hides of his cattle. Did – did he ask you last night, Jude, and maybe you half-promised–?'

She nodded slowly and Esteban's hands tightened on her arms. 'Why, I figured– But, sure we know what he is like and you don't *have* to–'

Her glance lifted now and though her lips curved bravely, there was no answering smile in the gentian eyes.

'We do know what Roy Holman is like, and you are partly right. But he is not the whole trouble and I – I was prepared to – to do what he asked for – for your sake as well as mine, Steve. Oh, it is no more than thousands of other women do–' She contrived a quick, warmer smile. 'Maybe the boot is on the other foot, and it is Roy we should be feeling sorry for – married to a Valdés! We who can hate as fiercely as we can love... No! I don't hate him, not yet!

'A week back, two days even, I was willing to go through with this, even though I had no intention of satisfying Holman's ungovernable impatience–'

'Look, *chica,* if it is like this, we will not have you do it! No longer do we live according to outmoded custom! The marriage of convenience; the bridegroom chosen for the bride! *Por dios!* These things are of the past, I tell you, *chica!* If today our father were alive, then perhaps...' In his sincerity Esteban reverted to the more traditional phraseology, even interspersing his words with Spanish endearments scarcely used between them since their childhood.

'Look!' he said again, one hand releasing her arm and indicating the heap of money. 'Maybe this is not enough to go very far, but like I told you, there will be more. Señor Latimer is willing to pay. He has the dinero but not the land–'

'But if I were to contract myself in marriage with – with Roy, there would be no

109

doubt, Steve. Everything would be taken care of, all our debts paid. Oh, make no mistake, *chico*, Mr Roy Holman would be only too pleased, not only to forgo a dowry, but to provide–'

Esteban stood back a pace, shaking his head. 'Maybe I had not thought sufficiently about this until now, Judith. Maybe I have been walking about with a blindfold and fooling myself that yours was but a small price to pay to save the Valdés' name. If you could only learn to–'

'Learn to love *him*?' She smiled, and her face, framed by the shining black hair, held an almost bitter-sweet expression. She moved across to the *cajoneria* and poured a glass of tequila, drinking it down quickly.

'I've never seen you use a glass of wine like this before.'

'I have never felt quite as I do now.'

'You mean – Holman?'

'Not Holman alone, no. You see, Steven, I am already in love with someone else. That was what I meant when I said just now, "a week back, two days even"...'

He stared at her incredulously, striving to grasp the full significance of this dramatic revelation as she moved slowly back to where he stood.

'A bombshell, is it not?' she smiled. 'Sure, and it was like that for me, just two days back, Steve, when you rode in here with a man called Ventura...'

'*Ventura?*' The single name seemed to be wrung from Esteban's throat in agony. His dark-skinned face looked yellowish now in the evening window-light.

'What is so wrong, Steve–?'

'Ventura!' he repeated. 'Are you sure of this thing, *chiquita:* are you sure it is this – this bounty hunter you love?' He did not have to wait for any affirmative word. The answer lay there in her shining face, in the depths of her eyes and in the soft, tremulous curve of her lips.

'*Beatísima María,*' he breathed gently and turned away from his sister's searching glance...

With two strong slugs of whisky inside him, Mike Santeely's colour slowly returned. He gazed at the man across from him still unable it seemed, to believe the evidence of his senses. Once or twice his glance strayed to the blanket covered shape lying as still as a butchered steer on the puncheon floor. He reached for the shot glass, unaware that it was empty for a second time.

Ventura tilted the bottle, sloshing liquor into both glasses. 'Drink it, Santeely, you've earned it!'

'I – I have earned it?' He caught some indefinable expression in the steel-grey eyes of the man who had saved him; not humour perhaps, but a glint of something not far removed from grim satisfaction.

'He died like a fool, Santeely, so save your regrets. A man like this contributes nothing to the world from the time he is born to the time he dies. What was he? A hired gunman if ever I saw one. Taking orders blindly, killing blindly, coldly, with no more thought or feeling for himself than for his victims–'

'He – he – was Gil James – foreman–'

'Sure. I heard that much. Roy Holman's gun-dog. One of Holman's tools to help lever his master to the heights and look down on the suckers and weaklings he broke–' Ventura stopped suddenly and into his drawn, glistening face, crept the merest shadow of a smile.

'Pardon me for making a speech. Next time I sound off you'd best slug me with that bottle.'

'Whoever you are, mister, I owe you more than I can ever repay. As for speech-makin', go right ahead an' spout. Mebbe in between whiles, I can catch my own breath.'

Ventura built another quirly and wiped a match alight, giving the nester his name. 'Sometimes I collect bounty money – when I'm lucky enough to haul in some desperado the law hasn't hooked.'

Santeely frowned in thought. 'Wasn't it you who caught up with one of the notorious Ketchum's gang, round about a year ago, I seem to remember? But how come you're back in the Yerba Valley? More important still, by what miracle did you ride *here* – tonight of all nights…?'

'Mebbe it was a miracle at that,' Ventura agreed gravely. 'For just a while back I hadn't even heard of you. I guess it was kind of an impulse, a hunch if you like.' And then he recounted his recent talk with Marshal Baumann, culminating in his riding out and following the tracks made by Dulcie Randell's buckboard, and finally arriving at the scrub-bordered creek.

'It sure takes some beating, how you could follow a trail all that way,' Santeely murmured, 'still more, find your way here – less'n you picked up the tracks of *my* hoss.'

'No. By the time I figured out some kinda explanation for all that sign, it was coming on to dusk.' Ventura's faint smile appeared. 'Hunters hate quitting a trail, I guess, 'specially when they're feelin' lucky. So I rode on a bit, lookin' around and figurin' if this *was* the Jarvis strip, then likely your cabin would be around some place. Just a question of whether I could pin-point it.' He drew deeply on the cigarette. 'I saw the light presently, but when I got down here, something sure smelled, an' it wasn't victuals cooking over a camp-fire!

'A hoss was tethered in amongst the trees, but I didn't know at that time who it belonged to, 'cepting it was Arrow. But–' He paused a moment to finish his drink. 'Reckon I heard enough today, Mike, to know Holman's bin pushin' you, mebbe others as well. Aside of that, I met him myself coupla days back. Now you can understand why I came up quietly.'

For the first time Santeely allowed himself a tight-lipped smile. 'Sure! an' I can thank my stars you were not only curious about Dulcie, but you also had the nerve, the ability – I – I just don't know how you beat him. It's–'

'It's just so much water down the river now, I reckon, though Holman likely will raise Cain.' He shrugged resignedly. 'We'll just haveta take care of that when it comes. Meanwhile, put the whole thing behind you – if you can. Sure, it's not easy! Nor is killin' a man – even a hombre like this one!'

He stood up and surveyed the plain but well-kept living room with eyes that in fact absorbed no more than a minimum of detail.

'It's not the first time something like this has happened,' he said quietly, 'and mebbe it won't be the last.' For a moment or two he seemed held in a reverie of the past. Then he turned abruptly and withdrew his gun, ejecting the spent shell and feeding a fresh one into the empty chamber.

'What about–?' Santeely's gaze moved

across to the covered body of Gil James.

'I'll haveta tote him in to Latigos, just to keep the record straight. Not that Baumann will like this one little bit–'

'If it's a matter of a witness – swearing you saved my life, and James went for his gun first...'

Ventura nodded. 'I guess Baumann will want a statement from you too. Best thing you can do is ride back with me...'

'Sure I will, but you'll have somethin' t'eat first, an' a cup of coffee?'

'My appetite's not so good, right now, Mike.'

'No more is mine, but a few soda crackers and java?'

''Stá bueno! I'll go round up James' horse and mebbe you'll give me a hand tying him on?'

It was nearing ten o'clock when the two riders trotted their mounts down Main, approaching town from the stage road.

Men on the sidewalks glanced incuriously at first and then halted to stare more closely as lamplight revealed a third horse trailing behind on a long lead rein. Instead of a rider, the saddle held a blanket-wrapped shape securely lashed in position and few of the onlookers failed at a second glance to realize that this was no pack-horse carrying supplies.

Moreover the man aboard the steel-dust

115

was Ventura; his companion, Mike Santeely, a rare enough visitor to town by all standards. And to men accustomed to judging the signs, it was noticeable that both riders held themselves unnaturally straight and taut.

When they reined in outside the marshal's office, a small crowd quickly converged onto the spot. One man, stepping forward, peered closely at the rear horse with its unmistakable burden. 'Bigawd!' he muttered huskily, 'it's sure enough Gil James' hoss!'

Ventura's voice sliced through the ensuing babble like a knife through butter. 'Anyone know where's the marshal at?'

Two-three of them swung their gazes across to the office, seeing at once that it was in darkness.

Henry Levistone, who owned and ran the biggest hardware store in town, spoke up. 'Not ten minutes back he was along at the Trailsman. Usually reckons to have a drink around about now.'

Mark Hardacre, a young lawyer, laid his quick glance on Santeely's grimly-drawn face. 'Is this really Gil James' body you're bringing in, Mr Santeely?'

Mike nodded, wondering how much information, if any, Ventura was prepared to give out at this stage. But a sudden movement on the crowded boardwalk caught Santeely's eye and lamplight winked on the deputy's star pinned to Ollie Kirby's vest.

'Hey! What's goin' on hyar you fellas?' Kirby shoved forward at the moment Ventura leaned from the saddle and tied his lead rein to the rack.

'That's Holman's foreman, Kirby,' he told the deputy, jerking his head towards the burdened horse. 'Keep an eye on things while we see the marshal, will you?'

'Hey! Wait a minute! What–'

But the other had gigged his horse forward, apparently oblivious of Ollie's somewhat incoherent protests and, taking his cue from Ventura, Mike Santeely spurred his own mount alongside, both riders heading down street to the Trailsman Saloon.

Sensational news most generally travels ahead of itself like a forest fire, and as soon as the two men pushed through the batwings, they knew that a few sparks at least had blown into the saloon already.

'What kinda trouble is it now, Ventura?'

Baumann shot the question from where he stood at the bar, speculative glance on the hard-visaged bounty hunter and his unlikely companion.

'Trouble, Will? Who said there was trouble?'

Baumann wiped his drooping moustache, flicked his gaze from one to the other. 'I don't rightly know – yet, but someone just this moment called out you an' Santeely has

117

humped in a body – I was coming right out–'

'Kirby's out there, Marshal, with his sights lined on things–'

'Quit stallin'!' Baumann snapped and pushed away from the bar. 'Come to that, what are you doin' along with this trouble-shooter, Santeely?'

Suddenly impatient, Ventura gestured with his hand; tired of these verbal gambits, tired of the whole damnable business.

'Mebbe we'd best talk this over in your office, Will, an' give you the score.'

'I'd shore be glad for somebody to tell me.'

'Have it your way! Me an' Mike here have brought Gil James' body in, for the coroner's benefit and yours, I guess. He tried to murder Mr Santeely, an' I had to kill him, is all!'

Over to the gambling tables the roulette wheel slowed to a stop. Even the clicking of poker chips and the rattle of dice slowly subsided and merged into the last fading note of the tinny piano.

'What was that again?' Baumann asked softly.

'It's like Mr Ventura said.' Santeely's voice, low-pitched, yet sounded surprisingly firm. 'James was going to shoot me in cold blood – my hands tied behind me! Mr Ventura arrived just in time – but even then James drew first!' He shook his head. 'I've never seen the like of it, Marshal Baumann!'

The lawman seemed unable to trust himself to further speech at the moment. He merely jerked his head and moved towards the door, the two men following quietly behind...

CHAPTER VII

CUERVO!

'So that's everythin' you can tell me?' Baumann rose from his desk, brought the coffee pot over from the stove and refilled the three cups.

'You got any idea what this is likely to start, Ventura? Why couldn't–'

'You would sooner have had Mike murdered, me likewise, than that I should shoot a killer?'

'We don't *know* Gil James was a killer–'

Ventura slammed his hand down on the desk, making the coffee spill over from the cups.

'I'm sorry, Will, but there was nothing else to be done. We've already told you James came over to do murder on Holman's instructions. He admitted it, but this was when he figured he only had Santeely to deal

119

with and him already helplessly tied up.'

Baumann opened his mouth to speak just as Ollie Kirby tromped into the room.

'Doc Clinthrow's examined the body, Will, an' the coroner's fixed fer an inquest tomorrow at two o'clock. We gotta show up then along with Mr Ventura an' Mr Santeely.'

'Did Judd say we could tote James out to Arrow tonight?'

'Sure. I got him in Hatch's spring-wagon, Will. All set when you're ready.'

'Guess mebbe I'd better make me a last will an' testament before I go!'

Santeely said, 'But Holman cain't do anythin' to *you*, Marshal. Why, the whole county—'

'Mebbeso.' Baumann's smile was grimly sardonic. 'But if he don't try killin' me he can do the next best thing, which he surely will – run me outa town!'

'That's foolish talk, Will. Holman's only one man in the Yerba Valley. You're elected by the townspeople right here in Latigos.'

'Then if that's what you figger, Ventura, it jest shows you don't know much about the kind of power a man like Roy Holman can swing. I tell you he's behind most everythin' that happens in San Pablo County – 'specially when it comes to politics. Wait till you've seen him fer one thing.'

'I have, Will.'

'When? You didn't ever say you'd met him!'

'I didn't figure it important enough to mention,' Ventura replied coolly. 'My impressions were of an uncouth, uneducated, loud-mouthed braggart; likely enough a criminal to boot, but cunning like a fox.'

From the corner, Ollie Kirby chuckled. 'That sure is tellin' the world, Mr Ventura, only... I wouldn't go spoutin' that kinda *habla* outside!'

Ventura came up from his chair, whirled on the others in the room. 'He's got you all buffaloed, is the trouble! Sure, I know it's tough for you an' Kirby, Will! D'you think I don't know *something* at least of what these big apes can do to a man, whether he's a duly elected Peace Officer or – or a struggling homesteader?'

'Quite a speech,' Baumann mocked. 'Now what you goin' to do. Take the two-hun'ed bucks Ollie brought back an' ride on?'

'No, Will,' he said presently, 'because for one thing, like you just heard, I shall have to give evidence to the coroner. Secondly, I'm not ridin' on until it's made plain to Holman that if he's figurin' on startin' a feud, then *I'm* the one to start something with, not the Marshal of Latigos!'

Baumann had the grace to colour. 'I hope I ain't too fat-headed t'apologize fer what I said.'

'Skip it, Marshal. In any case, mebbe there's other reasons why I don't aim to pull out – yet!'

'Well,' Santeely put in quietly. 'I know now what it feels like when you only got a few minutes to live, and I'm already to admit it had me scared sick. But this man risked his own life to save mine – me, a complete stranger! Whatever Ventura does is jake by me an' I'll ride along with him no matter what – even if he's fixin' to brace the whole of Arrow!'

Baumann gnawed his lower lip, considering two possible alternatives, three maybe. He could quit, of course, for reasons of 'health,' try to find another job some place else. Or he could openly offer to side with Holman and rely on the big man to frame Ventura 'legally' or otherwise dispose of– He checked abruptly, appalled and disgusted at the idea of throwing Ventura to the wolves. Thirdly? To face up to things as squarely as possible, even Arrow, and give the man who had bested Gil James all the aid he could – though it might mean winding up under a marker on boothill! For if Roy Holman ever found difficulty in ridding himself of an enemy by political chicanery, then he would not hesitate to use the time-tested and usually conclusive alternative. That he had lost his ace gun-fighter through this made *modus operandi* might be an added inducement in employing a hired gun-hand rather than a smart-aleck lawyer.

Baumann shoved his hat far back and scratched the top of his sparsely covered head, suddenly realizing, amongst other things, that even without Ventura's intervention, the law would still have had Santeely's death to deal with. Sooner or later the pot would have begun to boil. It was just that this hombre had the knack of hastening the cooking along. What had he said only last night? Something about things simmering under the lid, and, by Gregory! it sure looked that way, if it was true that Holman had been after the Jarvis strip and was even prepared to kill for it!

Was there any tie-up, then, between this business tonight and actions like the poisoning of Starcross's trail-herd, for instance? But Will Baumann's mind refused to advance further beyond that point. There were too many unknown quantities and not enough facts.

'If you're fixin' to stick your neck out,' he told the bounty hunter at last, 'you might live longer wearin' a deppity's badge. Sure! I know that don't stop a lawman bein' dry-gulched some quiet place, but at least it gives a man *some* authority. Moreover, even a professional gunsel ain't allus so keen to rub out a Peace Officer.'

'Mebbe I'll take you up on that, Will. I'd

sure admire to watch Holman's face when he sees me wearin' a star!'

Baumann reached down into the bottom drawer of his desk, came up with a badge in his hand and placed it on the top. 'Whenever you want, I'll swear you in,' he offered. 'Meanwhile, you better take this dinero an' sign the official receipt. Ollie! You got everythin' in that satchel?'

'Sure have, Will, includin' a batch of dispatches fer you from the courthouse.' Kirby dumped the satchel's contents onto the table and Baumann checked the money and handed it to Ventura in exchange for the signed and dated receipt.

'Which reminds me. What about Dillis?' Ventura inquired.

'Kirby says he ain't likely to be up for trial for a few days on account the District Attorney's scratchin' around for further evidence. That right, Ollie?'

'Sure. You'll find all them details in Digby's letter when you get to it.'

'Mebbe I'd best do that right now, if you'll excuse me, gentlemen?'

'Sure.' Ventura looked across at Santeely. 'I'm heading for the Bosque House restaurant. You care to join me?'

'I guess so, if...' he paused a moment, switching his attention back to Baumann.

'Somethin' just occurred to me, Marshal, about...'

'What's on yore mind?'

'I – well, I guess it concerns Ventura here as well as you and Deputy Kirby. What I'm thinkin' is that mebbe you'll be making a report on this – this...'

'On the shootin' of James? Sure, I got to! First off we have the nice little chore of tellin' Holman himself. Then a written report for San Pablo by tomorrow's stage. But what–'

'What he's getting at, Will,' Ventura murmured from the door, 'is, let's leave out the fact I was following the tracks of a buckboard. Miss Randell doesn't figure in this at all; why cain't it be left that way?'

A light dawned in Baumann's eyes and he pondered a moment, traversing his gaze from one to the other. 'I guess it's like you say. That bit jest don't signify. No need fer us to go draggin' in such things, I reckon. What say, Ollie?'

'Why, surely, Will. What's bin said in this office is jest *our* business, less'n it's got a bearin' on the shootin'. In this instance, like you say, it don't connect.'

Santeely swallowed hard. 'My grateful thanks, gentlemen. Seems like I sure am indebted to a few folks right now! Mebbe one day I'll have a chance to do the same thing for one of you.

'There is another thing, Marshal. Miss Randell's husband has threatened to come here – I cain't go into it all but he's the kind to make trouble. If that happens then the whole town'll know.'

'They won't know anythin' from us, Santeely, more'n they do at present,' Baumann promised.

'Thanks a lot, Marshal, an' you too, Mr Kirby.' He turned to Ventura, but Baumann's next words held the two men.

'Somethin' just caught my eye in this letter! Digby says they questioned Hank Dillis pretty thoroughly, but he wouldn't talk. Only thing was that he kinda let slip a name an' then swore afterwards he'd never used it!'

'What was the name, Will?'

'Seems he mentioned a hombre called Steve Crowley – or Crow – some such handle. That mean anything to you?'

'I guess not. Doesn't sound familiar to me. Mebbe you got an old dodger out on him?'

Baumann shook his head. 'I don't think so, but we'll go through them presently. This Steve Crowley *could* be another member of the Butler gang or some kinda contact.'

'Sure, it's possible.' Ventura nodded to the two lawmen before stepping outside with Santeely. Within a short while they were seated at a corner table in the restaurant of the Bosque House.

'So it's not just that Holman's out for land, Mike,' Ventura said later, as the two of them sat over coffee. 'He sicced James on you because you witnessed a killing?'

'Two killings!' Santeely nodded. 'You must've heard some of what James said when you were outside the cabin door, but I figgered on filling in the gaps for you.'

'Shoot.'

The nester rolled a quirly and handed the Bull Durham sack and papers across to Ventura.

'Two-three months back, I reckon it would be, sometime in March, anyway. Starcross had made a real early round-up, not just brandin' calves, but cutting out a beef herd for market. Seems like Glen Summers, the Starcross strawboss, had recently hired a coupla extra hands. Two brothers name o' Fletcher...'

'I heard what James said about *that*. According to him they "doctored" this trail herd, presumably on the orders of Gil James or Holman himself. Then I guess they demanded a larger share of the cake and Holman had to get rid of them.'

Santeely nodded, put a match to their cigarettes and leaned across the table.

'Seeing that the Jarvis strip is like the space between two forks of a branch – the forks bein' Arrow land – it means whenever I ride to town or any place else for that matter, I gotta cross Arrow territory at some point.'

'Sure. I can see that, Mike.'

'Well, it was right after Starcross had reported the whole of their trail herd dead from locoweed poisoning. I was headin' for San Pablo an' I saw some riders two-three miles off disappearing into a gully. They were Arrow riders, but even at that distance I could see they'd got a coupla men in the middle, hands tied behind 'em.

'Something kept whisperin' for me to stay clear; that it wasn't my business, but I still rode on and got in close enough for a look-see.'

'You never spoke about this to the marshal or the law in San Pablo?'

'No. What was the use? They'd 'a' sworn I was lyin' or mistaken. There were seven-eight of them against one of me.

'I guess I felt pretty sick when I saw James shoot both the men dead, never a chance to defend themselves. Oh, I reckon they deserved to die for what they did to Starcross, but – well, mebbe I know now how they musta felt, hands tied behind them, eyes looking into the barrel of Gil James' .45.' The nester finished his coffee and dragged on his cigarette before continuing.

'This section they picked was pretty rough country, unworked and mostly deserted. I saw them dump those two bodies into a

128

deep ravine, Ventura, and I figgered it was time I got the hell out of it.'

'And they spotted you?'

'I reckon so. Mebbe they were not certain at first, and I was some long way off by this time. But likely James and the others got to figgerin' it was me. I was sure expectin' trouble, but nothing happened! Weeks went by and I spent some sleepless nights trying to figure out what chance there was of the law believin' *my* evidence, and finally decided against risking it.'

'You figured Holman would start gunning for you?'

'I guess so. The odd thing was, when he made his cash offer for the strip there was no mention or hint of anything beyond he needed the land – some vague talk about developing an irrigation system, was all. So that by now I was beginning to doubt I had been seen near the ravine, or if so, likely they hadn't recognized me.' He stubbed the cigarette out and folded his arms on the table, glancing quickly around the nearly deserted dining-room before going on.

'There are reasons why I don't intend quitting the valley or bein' kicked out. I'm not a fighting man, Ventura, as you can guess, but–'

'Mebbe for one thing, you hope the day might arrive when Miss Randell will be free?'

Santeely shot his benefactor a keen glance. 'Why shouldn't I admit it to you, the man who saved my life tonight?' He smiled thinly. 'I guess it's not guts, though; it's just that I'm ornery-minded. So I refuse Holman's price an' then last Monday he raises the ante like I told you, and James tells me it's the final offer!

'It wasn't until tonight, when he taunted me–'

'Sure. It proves they *do* know you witnessed the two killings, and Holman's kinda scary that sooner or later you're goin' to talk!'

The nester nodded. 'Looks like I'm still a bad risk. Way I see it, soon as they tote James' body to Arrow and Holman finds his scheme misfired, he's goin' to think up something to fix me good an' quick. Y'see, Ventura, he's still in the clear even if the marshal should question him. All he's gotta do is deny all knowledge that James was gunnin' for me.'

'Yeah. Even with me as a witness to some of the conversation, the evidence'd be too insubstantial for a jury to convict a man on, least of all one with Holman's influence. Bearing that in mind, it's possible he might try getting you in some other way – false evidence with some bit of legal flim-flam to help things along. You got to walk mighty careful from now on, Santeely!

'There's just one other thing,' Ventura added. 'How d'you figure Holman's reasons for destroying that trail herd, always supposin' he really did get the Fletcher hombres planted at Starcross?'

He signalled the waitress for the bill, and when the girl had gone, Santeely answered: 'I've lived in this country all my life, even if I haven't got much to show for it.' He gestured wearily. 'Folks'll tell you I keep to myself, an' it's true. Why, I've talked with you, Mr Ventura, more'n I've done with anyone around here, and the fact is I know little enough about Starcross and how they live. But town gossip says that Esteban and his sister Judith have been goin' through a tough time raisin' enough dinero to keep things going.

'My opinion, for what it's worth, *amigo,* is that Holman aims to break them financially, then come to their rescue, trading this "help" for a handsome wife. Once this is done, he'll be virtually in control of all their grazing land and water. How does that strike you?'

'It figures all right, Mike. One bold stroke and he's got mebbe nine-tenths of the entire valley – a dynasty on its own. And, with a beautiful wife, he can move to Santa Fe and really start in climbing...'

'And there's no one big enough to stop him!'

Ventura's smile held no more warmth than a winter's scene. 'I wouldn't bet on that, Mike. A Sharp's .50 slug can stop a bull buffalo dead in its tracks.'

Santeely's eyes rounded in shocked surprise. 'You're not figgerin'–? No!' He shook his head emphatically. 'You're no bushwhacker, *amigo,* on that I'd stake my life!'

'A figure of speech, mebbe. Far as I'm concerned, Holman can pull all the dirty deals he wants, in order to get the governorship. But I can promise you one thing, Mike, he's not grabbing Starcross!'

For the space of a few seconds Santeely could only stare. He recalled the casually dropped information in the marshal's office concerning this man who had again brought in a dangerous outlaw. Now, in the level grey eyes, he read something of the implacable purpose reflected there, a controlled strength lending this man's words such absolute conviction that it was difficult to believe his bold claim would not be accomplished somehow.

'Well, I wouldn't know how you go about cuttin' a man like that down to size, but you can sure count me in. If you figger there's some way I can help, all you gotta do is say.'

'Thanks, Mike. Mebbe you *can* help, in a way, though likely you'll get to wonderin' what it's all about–'

'See here, *amigo.* You don't haveta explain

132

things till you're good an' ready. There's no strings attached if I can be of any use. Don't you reckon I've got every reason to trust the man as saved my hide?'

'Mebbe so. But what if I needed to use your cabin or barn?'

'They're yours for as long as you want!'

'Even if it means hiding someone away up there – mebbe even kidnapping?'

'I won't be askin' questions, I'll be *helping*, even if you're fixin' to snatch the marshal, or – hide away a – a outlaw!'

'*Gracias*, again.' Ventura glanced at the wall clock whose hands showed nearly eleven-thirty. 'I think I could use your help, Mike, right now if you're willing to do some night riding.'

'I'm used to it. Is that all?'

'Not quite, so you better not say "yes" until you've heard the whole thing.'

'Yes,' Santeely said, and smiled.

He leaned against the tree trunk, gazing out from the shadows onto the trail along which Santeely would ride. A new moon sailed in the jewel-sprinkled sky, adding its pale light to the starglow silvering the parkland.

Carefully, more from habit, Ventura lit the quirly between his lips, shielding the flame, afterwards covering the glowing ember with the palm of his cupped hand.

Supposing he was wrong about all this? It

was a possibility that couldn't be overlooked. And supposing he was taking far too much on himself? Likely he was, at that, only now, at least, there was a deputy's star pinned to his shirt under the open brush jacket. Baumann had sworn him in, gratefully it had seemed, and like Santeely, had refrained from directing a barrage of questions.

Yes, there was little doubt that Esteban had sought him out in the first place, because of a singular interest in the Hank Dillis affair. For what other reason could he have picked on Ventura and invited him to Starcross? But that in itself was not sufficient evidence, by far, to prove that Valdés was in any way mixed up with a bunch of desperadoes. True enough. But there was something else infinitely more conclusive, a clue which apparently as yet only Ventura had spotted. According to Sheriff Digby's letter, Hank Dillis had inadvertently spilled a name, a name that had sounded like Steve Crowley or Steve Crow. Likely, as soon as he had realized his slip, Dillis had buttoned up again, maybe flatly denying he had ever mentioned another man's name. But Digby or his deputies had not been asleep, and had figured it worth while to pass on the information to all Law Enforcement officers in the county, including the Marshal of Latigos.

It hadn't struck Ventura until later on over

the meal with Santeely. And there it was, staring them all in the face! Esteban was the Spanish for Steven and *Cuervo* the Spanish for Crow! So, Esteban José Cuervo y Valdés became Steve Crow, when or *if* he rode with Torch Butler's gang!

Fantastic as the idea had seemed at first sight, Ventura had worked at it, seeking in his mind for reasons, motives – an explanation that would fit the situation to perfection, and he was sure now he had found it...

It was nearing two o'clock, and the night sky still clear and brilliant, when Ventura moved across to the steel-dust and stepped into leather. Gently he gigged the horse out onto the trail and across to the single lance-leaved cottonwood marking the rendezvous, and waited patiently as the two approaching riders drew near.

Shortly he kneed the gelding forward, narrowing the distance until the new-comers were no further than twenty yards.

'Ventura?' Esteban's voice, sharp-edged with uncertainty, stabbed through the muted sounds of night. 'Santeely gave me your note, and I came only because you said it concerned my sister and was, maybe, a matter of life and death! What fool talk *is* this, Señor Ventura? I want to know and damned fast!'

'So you shall, Esteban.' The words were

soft as a rippling breeze. He reined over to Valdés' right stirrup with such naturalness and ease of movement that it never occurred to the Starcross owner he was flanked on either side.

He thrust forward in the saddle searching Ventura's shadowed face in half-puzzled anger. Here was the very man whom Butler had said would have to be taken care of. The man whose continued existence might well prove more than a thorn in their flesh. This dangerous hombre for whom Judith had quietly yet so passionately proclaimed her love! Mother of God! What should he do now and why had Ventura, of all people, urged him to ride out here in the small hours along with Santeely?

But he was spared the necessity of deciding what course he should take, for, like a darting snake, Ventura's arm streaked out and there in his hand lay Esteban's gun, whipped from holster before even Valdés could move.

'Take it easy, Valdés, and you won't get hurt!' All softness had gone from the bounty hunter's voice. Now it was as hard as the steel in his eyes, the steel in his hand.

'What are you trying to do?'

'Mike!'

Santeely reached forward, grabbing the reins of Valdés' mount. In his right hand the homesteader held Ventura's gun, borrowed earlier for this very purpose.

'Listen, Valdés,' Ventura hissed. 'Like I said, you won't come to any harm if you do what you're told, *presto!* Mebbe you deserve to get hurt, mebbe you deserve to serve a term in jail.'

'What do you mean?' Esteban choked. 'Have you gone crazy?'

'Put your hands on the saddle-horn and keep 'em there!' Ventura had thrust the gun into holster and now in his hand was a length of rawhide.

'You can't get away with this! I'll have Marshal Baumann run you outa town, if you don't–'

'And if you don't keep quiet,' Ventura snarled, 'we'll do it the easy way and lay a gun across your head!'

Through the fog of Valdés' helpless fury and bewilderment ran a sliver of fearful doubt. And if he wanted to lay this ghost of uncertainty, then he must play it Ventura's way!

Obediently he allowed his wrists to be tied to the horn, bitterness in his eyes for these men who had tricked him into coming here. He strove hard to inflect his voice with a calmness he was far from feeling.

'Do you favour giving an explanation *before* the execution, or *after?*' he drawled.

Ventura smiled coldly. 'Maybe you'll live to thank me yet – *Mister Steve Crow!*'

CHAPTER VIII

PATTERN OF CONFUSION

Dawn's first light was a golden nimbus in the east when Ventura returned to the Bosque House, weary and travel-stained. He sluiced himself in cold water and carefully shaved and dressed.

It was eight o'clock by the time he had breakfasted, the town well astir. Several early shoppers intermingled with the business men and traders as stores, saloons and offices opened up in the eternal cycle of enterprise.

He built and fired his second quirly, strolled down to the marshal's office and found the door open to the morning sun. He stepped inside, seeing Baumann at the stove, pouring coffee. Loud snores from a corner bunk indicated that Ollie Kirby was still catching up on recent lost sleep.

'Mornin', Ventura. Coffee?' Baumann waved the pot over an empty tin cup.

'No thanks, Will. Just finished breakfast. Glad to see you're still alive! How did it go?'

The marshal came across from the stove, deposited his cup on the desk and stared

138

hard out of red-rimmed eyes.

'Don't look like you had much more sleep than me an' Ollie,' he commented with a meagre smile, and drank down half the coffee at a single gulp.

'Meaning that Holman kept you there half the night?'

'Wal, not quite. But by the time we'd gotten out there with James' body it was close on one o'clock. I guess we finally got away around 3 a.m., during which time Holman gave us the whole treatment.'

'Bad?'

The other nodded. 'More'n once I figgered he was goin' to bust himself, 'specially at the beginning. Fust off, he wouldn't believe it till he'd been out to the wagon an' looked for himself. Sure started in ravin' after that, demanding I should arrest Santeely, then you, and then the both o' you! Y'know, Ventura, Holman's the king-pin around here, and not just because he's tough an' got guns to back him up. He ain't gotten where he has in territorial affairs without a deal o' brains!

'Yet, when a hombre like that goes off half-cocked – wal...' the lawman shrugged. 'I guess after a while he began to see there wasn't a dam' thing he could do about it. Sure, he can fix things so's I don't get re-elected as marshal, but the fact remains, James cain't talk an' the only evidence is what you an' Santeely gave.

'No Peace Officer would hold either you or Mike, least of all issue a warrant fer your arrests, on account there ain't a dam' thing to show it wasn't self-defence like you claimed. Oh, he saw it that way after a time.' Baumann laughed grimly. 'I even asked him what he figgered the district attorney'd say when he heard Gil James'd bin shot.'

'What was that, Will?'

Baumann circled the desk and slumped wearily into his chair and grinned. 'Told him the D.A.'d be dam' pleased someone'd hadta kill such a gun-slinger an' mebbe in the long run it was savin' the county the expense of a trial!'

Ventura nodded. 'I guess he's got others out at Arrow to take James' place though? Santeely's in real danger I reckon, after what he told us – more especially what he told *me* in the Bosque House last night.'

'He have somethin' t'add, mebbe, to his statement?'

'Plenty! I'm not sure why he didn't come out with it to you an' Ollie. Mebbe for the same reason he's held silent all this while.'

'Silent about what?'

'Wasn't just a case of killing a nester for his land, Will. James was out to silence Santeely for witnessing a coupla killings.'

'I guess you know what you're sayin', *amigo?*'

Ventura smiled and flicked open his brush jacket to reveal the law badge. 'I'm a deputy, remember? That's why I figure you should know about Santeely. By sheer chance he stumbled upon a bunch of Arrow riders, led by Gil James, right after that Starcross trail herd had been poisoned. They had the Fletcher boys along and shot them down in cold blood.'

'The hell you say! But this could be vital evidence—'

'Hold on, Will. You got the same thing there as happened last night – two or more men's word against the one.'

Rapidly Ventura sketched in the details as Santeely had described them, and Baumann was forced to admit that if the story were true – and Santeely had no apparent reason to lie – many things which had been obscure were now clear.

'Sure!' Baumann thumped his desk, startling the recumbent Kirby into complete wakefulness. 'It gives us the answer to why the herd was killed, as well as *who* was responsible, an' bigawd, I shore am beginning to see some daylight...'

Ventura leaned back against the wall. 'Much good the knowledge'll do us at the moment, Will. Nothing could be proved against Holman, not even if you recovered those bodies which by now are no more than a pile of bleached bones.'

Kirby swung his legs over the side of the bunk. 'Sounds like I bin missin' somethin' important?'

'The marshal likely'll wise you up, Ollie. Meanwhile I got a chore to do.' Ventura resettled the gun-belt around his hips, tugged at the brim of his hat, and pushed away from the wall.

'Ain't you tellin' us where yo're goin'?' Baumann said. 'Besides, don't forget the inquest's at two o'clock. Yo're a deppity now – remember?'

'Sure. But an unpaid one. Besides, this is kinda personal.'

Impatiently, Baumann shifted in his chair and stabbed a gnarled finger at Ventura. 'We know Mike Santeely's like a burr under the saddle to Arrow an' likely still in plenty danger. Wal, have you figgered out what could happen to *you*, the hombre as shot Roy Holman's foreman?'

'Several possibilities 've occurred to me,' the bounty hunter grinned, and with a brief nod stepped from the office, moving down-street towards the livery.

Some two hours later, he rode the steel-dust into Starcross and reined his mount in the direction of the white adobe ranch-house, before which Judith Valdés stood in deep conversation with the oldster, Charlie.

At once they glanced up, Williams instinctively stepping forward from the *pavimento* as the horseman approached.

'*Buenos dias*,' Ventura smiled, and removed the dusty stetson to incline his blond head in a slight bow.

'Good morning to you, Señor Ventura,' she replied, and could not but admire the way sunlight glinted on his hair and threw the planes of his face into sharp contrasts of light and shade.

'Mawnin',' the wrangler grinned, hand outstretched on bridle rein. 'I jest bin tryin' to tell Miss Judith thar ain't nothin' to worry over. Seems like–'

'Charlie! I'm sure Mr Ventura hasn't come here to listen to our troubles.'

'Why not, Miss Judith? Mebbe I can help you in some way?'

'Please forgive me for not inviting you to light down. I – I – we're a little worried...' She smiled belatedly as he stepped from the saddle, allowing Williams to lead the steel-dust across to the water trough.

'If it's about your brother, Miss Judith, let me assure you there's nothing to worry over; he's quite safe.'

'You know about Esteban? That he lit out last night without a word to anyone, not even Charlie or Glen, and that he's been gone all night?' Her lovely eyes had opened wide like deep blue flowers unfolding their dew-wet petals to the morning sun. 'B – but

143

how could you, *amigo,* unless perhaps you saw him in Latigos? I – I don't understand...'

'Of course you don't. It's why I've come to see you.' He paused for a moment, hat in hand, and the girl indicated the wooden chairs and table set out on the *pavimento.*

'Please forgive me again, Señor, and be seated while I see about some coffee.'

He watched her go into the house, and when she returned shortly he was standing by the table firing a cornpaper quirly.

'You don't mind?'

'Of course not,' she smiled. 'Coffee will not take long. Meanwhile...?'

'Meanwhile,' he echoed, dropping into the chair beside hers, 'like I said, nothin's happened to Esteban.'

'But what *is* it, Mr Ventura? Why can't you–?'

'Come to the point?' He regarded her soberly now, trying to assess her values, her strength of character, and unable in this close appraisal to remain oblivious to her physical attributes. The flame silk shirt blouse she wore did not entirely conceal the full and graceful sweep of her bosom, whilst reflecting some of its vivid colour onto the dark olive of her cheeks; and the divided riding skirt, whilst decorously reaching to boot-tops, was soft enough to hint at the lissom shapeliness beneath. Maybe, he thought, the desert rose tinge in her cheeks was not all reflected from the silken *camisa*.

'First,' he said quietly, 'will you answer *me* a few questions, Miss Judith? There's one-two things I haveta be sure about an' I reckon you can help me if you will.'

'Surely.' She arose, and as Josefa appeared from the house, took the tray from the girl, setting it on the table. 'What is it you would know?'

'*Do you trust me, Judith?*' Though the question was voiced softly enough, it was couched with such directness and held such latent possibilities that for a long moment she could only return his steady gaze, looking deeply into those eyes which could so swiftly chill with the cold of ice.

'What right have I got even to ask such a thing?' he added, 'or by what right...?'

'...do you use my first name? Is that what is in your mind, Ventura? Then let me say this! Do not misinterpret my hesitation. I – there is a great deal I could say, perhaps, but let it suffice that you may...' She coloured slightly '...that I *do* trust you implicitly!' She turned away to gaze out over the tawny, rolling grass beyond the buildings. 'It is something that a woman feels, Señor, in her heart.' Then suddenly she smiled and the web was broken. She filled two cups from the pot, placing a sugar bowl at his hand.

'You are not satisfied, Ventura? Then if you

would understand more deeply, ask me your questions and I will speak the truth as I know it – as you would say, with no strings attached!'

'That's the second time those words 've bin used lately. But *gracias, Señorita,* for your generous answer. Right now, I want you to tell me about Esteban.'

'What – about him?'

He sugared the coffee, stirring the thick liquid thoughtfully. 'Anything, Judith, anything – well, unusual that might 've happened lately, mebbe even within the last day or two.'

'Why, there's–' She stopped suddenly, aware now of a growing significance in all this. Only for a brief moment longer did she paused and then lift her head with an unself-conscious pride, as though to face the truth whatever it was, whatever it might cost.

'I – I'm not sure this is what you mean, Ventura, maybe it is. But only yesterday morning Steve rode out early, before dawn, saying nothing except to tell Charlie he was meeting a cattle-buyer.'

'Do you know where he went or who this man is, Judith?'

Her glance dropped to the shapely, sun-burned hands in her lap. 'He was – vague about it. Mentioned only that it was some place beyond San Pablo and that the stockman's name was Latimer. He said that Latimer was a Coloradoan rancher with herds of pure-bred shorthorns and that he needed graze and water and was willing to pay.

'He – Esteban – was gone most of the day and must have ridden much. It would be around five or six o'clock when he rode in, tired and dusty. Yet he – he seemed elated at first, and I felt that something way out of the ordinary had happened.

'Then, after he had told me about this buyer needing graze, he pulled a leathern poke from his coat and emptied it out in front of me!'

'The contents being – money?'

Again her quick glance came at him and moved away. She nodded. 'Yes. Eleven hundred dollars which Steven allowed was the cattleman's advance payment for a year's lease of a section of our range.' She looked at him almost pleadingly, desperately anxious to fathom the mystery, yet mindful of her pledge to trust him.

'Has Esteban bin on any similar kind of journey recently, Judith? I mean like ridin' some place, meeting up with someone you don't know, mebbe 've never met?'

She felt suddenly as though she were walking the edge of a high, narrow trail, whose end lay out of sight beyond an outcropping. Maybe the trail petered out in a

147

tangle of broken country or even came to an abrupt finish at the edge of a ravine. But whatever lay ahead, there could be no turning back. Retreat would not solve... Deliberately she forced her thoughts back from the realm of futile speculation, concentrating now upon Ventura's last question.

'Twice or three times perhaps over the last few months, since about the time we lost our trail herd, Esteban has done something like this. I have never thought about it before, Ventura, naturally, but—'

'And each time he's furnished you with – well, an alibi you couldn't very well check up on?'

'I – I guess so, if you put it that way. But you are not saying he has done anything–?'

He placed a hand on her arm in a gesture at once both reassuring and insistent.

'Wait a minute, Judith! I guess you're being plenty helpful, but this ... this isn't easy to say, *amiga*. Are you – is Holman...?'

He cursed softly as the girl's whole body stiffened. If he did not have the courage or the ability to finish saying what was in his mind, at least he met her gaze squarely, seeing the pain there as well as the flashing fury of a storm, where before had only been a gentle bewilderment. Tears sparkled on the dark lashes, not as droplets of dew, but more like the sparks from striking steel, and colour surged in her cheeks and in her agitation she was powerless to control the sharp rise and fall of her breasts.

It seemed to Ventura that, like a blacksmith, he had tried to hammer out a small girl's fragile bracelet and in the process had not merely damaged the trinket, but had weakened the child's simple trust.

He reached for his hat, stood gripping it awkwardly between his big-knuckled hands. 'I'm sorry, Judith. I guess I didn't—'

'Please stay,' she whispered softly, and when he looked again the storm had passed and only a blue tranquillity shone from her eyes.

'It – it's little use pretending that we are not hard-pressed for money,' she admitted, 'and – and Roy has been – seeking a wife for some time. He – he has asked me several times and – recently I gave him to believe...'

'I think I understand. Such a course would take care of the financial angle.'

'It sounds terrible, put into words,' the girl breathed softly. 'I – I wouldn't tell anyone else...'

He sat down again, dropped his hat onto a vacant chair, and leaned towards her. 'I sent a friend of mine here last night, Judith, to fetch Steve, if possible without anyone else's knowledge. And, in fact, it worked out that way, on account Charlie and the rest of your crew were in the bunkhouse likely asleep.'

'Then you really *do* know where Steve is?'

He nodded. 'You've still gotta trust me, Judith. Believe it or not, *I had to do this for you – for Steve's own safety!*'

The silence between them lengthened and Judith's glance drifted over bunkhouse and barns as she watched the wrangler at work, forking alfalfa into the corral. Shortly, she arose, pulling her gaze back to the man beside her.

'Please come into the living-room for a moment.'

'Sure.' He followed her into the flagged hallway, through into the big room where he had first met her less than three days since.

She turned and faced him, standing very erect, head proudly poised.

'You are trying to tell me that Esteban's story is a lie. That instead of making a deal over grazing rights, he has come by this money by some other means – *by some dishonest or criminal act!*' She paused for a moment before adding: 'Do you think, Señor, that the Valdés are rogues and cheats, that–?'

'Hold it, Judith! I didn't say that an' I sure don't believe it. Way I see things is that your brother's pulled some job to save this place, or at least give you a breathing space. Primarily I reckon he's done it to save you from Holman!'

'You mean…?'

150

Ventura said: 'He had to make a pretty tough choice a while back, Judith, when you lost that trail herd... What was the contract figure per head?'

She thought a moment. 'We had a contract to supply Fort Frazer with three hundred and twenty-five beef steers at twenty-two dollars a head, provided–'

'Sure. Provided they averaged the required weight. That means you lost somewhere around seven thousand bucks, an' ever since then Steve's bin tryin' to figure a way to recoup–'

'But, if what you say is true, this makes my brother a *criminal,* likely to be convicted!'

'It was to stop just such a thing happening that I ... I've got him tucked safely away. No one knows about this, certainly not the law! So he got away with it once! Next time he might not 've bin so lucky. This way – he's safe until...'

'Until – what, Ventura?'

He shrugged slightly, a wry smile on his lips.

'Mebbe until we can nail the hides of whoever poisoned your herd!'

'I – find it all so difficult to believe, or understand. You are trying to help us, *amigo,* risking a lot, maybe your life. You have – kidnapped Esteban to make sure he cannot commit another crime, yet you are wearing a deputy's badge?'

151

'Oh, that. Sure, I'd almost forgot. But mebbe it would help some if I told you what I told Marshal Baumann, that I was a lawman myself, once.'

He smiled, began pacing up and down the room with slow measured steps. 'In the eyes of the law, I guess I'd be – what do they call it? – conniving! But, there's more to it than that. In the first place, Esteban's not yet a "wanted" man. Like I said, no one knows about this outside the people directly concerned. Moreover, if or when we can get back those steers–'

'Get them back? But they were killed!'

'I know. But whoever did it is sure goin' to pay 'em back and with interest, and once you get the money Steve'll then be able to return that eleven hun'ed dollars he – er – *borrowed!*'

Judith sank into a chair at the huge Spanish mahogany table, and Ventura crossed over, placing his hand under her chin and gently raising the downcast head.

'It's a pattern of confusion, isn't it? Difficult of understanding. Believe me, Judith, there's a heck of a lot that's far from clear to me. Sure, I *know* a few things, but as yet they cain't be proved.' He moved away, commenced building a quirly, and no word passed between them until Ventura's cigarette was alight.

'There's something else I've gotta tell you,

amiga, before I go. Something you'll likely hear about fast enough.' It was no use trying to water it down, so he said quite simply: 'I had to kill Holman's ramrod last night. The inquest's at two o'clock this afternoon; just a formality, I guess.'

'James?' the girl whispered, 'you killed Gil James? Does that mean that you might be indicted for murder?'

He stared at her in amazement. Instead of a dozen wild questions, there was but the one, expressing fear for *him.* And in the dark blue, smoky eyes, where he might have expected to see revealed at least an un-equivocal disgust, lay only an anxious concern.

Abruptly and without preamble, she quit the chair to stand close in front of him. 'Tell me, Ventura! When this happened, were you a sworn-in deputy – engaged on law work?'

'No, *amiga.* But I'm in the clear if that's what you mean. 'Tis an open and shut case. James drew first an' I beat him, is all–'

'But what about Roy? Do you figure he will stand for this? Can't you see you'll be in danger?'

'You reckon Holman would bushwhack me just to even things up; send one of his gunsels after me?'

'You don't know him like I do,' she an-swered softly, gazing up into the sunburned face. 'If – if he had a mind to, he would not

153

hesitate to – kill, provided someone else pulled the trigger and he could be sure of remaining unsuspected!'

'Yet,' Ventura murmured, holding her shoulders lightly with both hands, 'you are willing to marry him!'

She made no move to draw away, but her glance quickly lowered.

'To be willing,' she reminded in a low whisper, 'is not always the same as wanting...'

'Then listen to me, Judith, an' heed what I say. *Don't* marry Holman, don't even *say* you will, not now nor in the future! I – I cain't ask you to make it a promise, for I've demanded too much of you already. But you've got to believe there's a mighty good reason!

'Why, mebbe we'll get those steers back for you, and if Fort Frazer won't buy 'em we'll find someone as will. What you gotta do, Judith, is hang on till we can straighten all this out, then there won't be any need to.'

'You give me fresh hope, *amigo.* And why should I not make you that promise? True, I don't know the answers to much of what you say, nor yet do I understand what you intend. But I have said that I trust you – even my brother's life is in your hands. Why should I not therefore do like you say in this matter?'

'Only that it's more'n any man has the

right to ask, 'less he's–'

'Rights!' There was a fine scorn in her voice, but gentled thoroughly by the smiling eyes and lips. 'You said that before,' she accused mockingly. 'But we are not discussing water or grass or boundaries. *Si!*' She threw back her head in pretended defiance and was for a moment all Spanish.

'If you want that I promise, then I do! And how do you like that, Señor Ventura! I will not marry Roy Holman until you give me your permission!'

He was the one to draw away first, jolted again by the sheer unpredictability of this lovely creature.

'It's more than I could've hoped, Judith,' he told her. 'I guess I figured this was one of those chores that had to be done...'

'...Yet one you did not expect would succeed,' she flashed. 'Well, *amigo,* maybe you underrate your talents. Indeed, I am sure! But tell me, please; how long must you keep my brother?'

'Mebbe not long, if he will give me his word.'

Ventura threw away the cigarette butt. 'If he won't do that, Judith, I'll have to hold him until – *Quién sabe?*'

'What – what would you do about this money? Is it really stolen, do you think?' She reached inside a shelf of the ornate *cajoneria,* lifting out the poke still filled with

155

gold and silver, and Ventura examined one or two of the coins.

'No way of identifying these–'

'*Plata!*' Judith exclaimed suddenly white-faced. '*The bank at Plata was robbed...!*'

CHAPTER IX

A FAST TRIP

'Quietly, *amiga,*' he told her, placing a hand on her soft mouth. 'Maybe, maybe not. We don't know for certain, yet, whether this is any of the money. Keep your own counsel for a while. Don't talk about this to anyone, not even your crew. Tell them Esteban will be away for a few days on this cattle deal. You can give your men their orders?'

'Yes. I often do. I – I'm sorry I – I called out like that! It was a – shock.'

'Don't cross the river till you come to it,' he advised, 'an' when you do, likely I'll be along to see you over safely. Right now I've gotta be ridin'.' He looked towards the mantelshelf on which stood a seventeenth-century French clock, the hands pointing to twelve-thirty. 'The inquest's at 2 p.m. Looks like I'll haveta burn leather.'

Silently she led the way outside, lifting an

156

arm in signal to the wrangler as he glanced their way. Before Charlie had halfway reached them with the led horse, Judith turned quickly. 'You will come again, *amigo*, as soon as you can?' It could have been a merely courteous invitation, or the words might have held some deeper significance.

'There's a few things need takin' care of today. Mebbe I'll not get through till late. Tomorrow...'

Williams was less than twenty yards away, handling the steel-dust, checking the sur-cingle as Judith's words came swift and low. 'This house is yours, *amigo mío. Vaya con Dios*...'

She remained there watching as he rode away over the grass to the distant road, finally disappearing from view where the mesa land stepped down towards the lower flats approaching town.

The inquest had been over very quickly, each man concerned having given his evidence concisely and with few interruptions from the coroner, Henry Levistone.

Baumann, Ventura, Santeely and Kirby had all said their piece as arranged previously between them. Basically, the story was true, but certain details had been omitted or glossed over for the sake of expediency. For the latter reason, it had earlier been decided between Levistone and the marshal that no useful purpose could be served in calling Holman or any of Arrow, officially. If they cared to show up in court they were at liberty to do so, but as the deceased had been identified last night by Doc Clinthrow as well as the law, and the manner of death established immediately, it had only remained for the details to be recorded and one or two obscure points clarified.

As it happened, no one had shown up from Arrow, and within a half-hour the verdict was proclaimed, the deceased having met his death as a result of attempting to murder another person.

The 'other person's' name was recorded, and on the marshal's recommendation a rider was added to the effect that the witness named Ventura had drawn *after* the deceased had so done and had, therefore, killed in self-defence.

It was also noted that the witness in question was completely exonerated from all blame in the eyes of the court (though he was neither on trial nor indicted) and that no further legalities were anticipated.

Outside the courtroom Ventura had a few snatched words with Santeely.

'How is he, Mike – safe enough?'

Santeely grinned. 'I reckon. That small alfalfa barn'd deceive most folks into figurin' it was only one storey high. Even was anyone to search the place they wouldn't find him.'

'He cain't get out?'

The nester shook his head. 'It's just like you left him and his horse is hidden out in the brush. Apart from that, he's bin cussin' most all the mornin' since breakfast, and yelling for you!'

'Let him sweat awhile,' Ventura replied. 'I'll be up there to see you sometime, Mike, but I don't know when. You keep a sharp watch-out, *amigo*, for any Arrow riders, though I doubt Holman would try pullin' the same stunt in the same place. That's not to say he mightn't try dry-gulchin' you *away* from the Jarvis strip.'

'I'll be careful,' Santeely said grimly, and stood watching as the bounty hunter crossed the old *placita* to where Marshal Baumann leaned against a hitching rack.

'Where's the nearest telegraph office, Will?'

'You jest had another bright idea, *amigo?*'

'Quit foolin', Will. The Atchison, Topeka an' Santa Fe's pushin' a railroad somewhere north o' here and I wanta get through to the capital *pronto!*'

'Plattville's the nearest place, Ventura. There's a telegraph hook-up along the spur to the main line. But you won't save any time by ridin' forty miles. Why not wait an' send it by coach tomorrow? Likely take several days for a reply, anyways.'

Ventura smiled. 'I'm figuring on a reply tonight, Will.'

'You gone crazy, son? That wire's buzzin' all day an' half the night not only with railroad messages, but–'

'What's the best trail for Plattville? I gotta get there fast an' I've no time to explain now!'

'All right. But you gotta have a priority to get a telegraph message clear through to the capital without waitin'!'

'I got one,' Ventura snapped. 'Now show me the trail. Which of those three forks on the stage road do I take?'

For a moment, Baumann stared in blank amazement. 'Bigawd, Ventura, I shore hope you know what yo're doin'! You take the right fork an' keep straight on. With luck you might make it by nine or ten o'clock tonight.'

'I'll make it by six or bust!'

'Say! What's so all-fired important you gotta kill a hoss, mebbe two? Who's gonna pay for this, *amigo?*'

'Mebbe Roy Holman,' Ventura growled, and swung up onto the boardwalk, heading fast for the livery.

Ten minutes later, Latigos was considerably surprised to see Ventura sweep out onto Main from the livery stables and go thundering through town aboard an ugly hammer-headed buckskin brute which Hatch Nimrod normally refused to hire out.

From the doorway of the marshal's office, Ollie Kirby gazed after the retreating, dust-enveloped rider, grinning a little as he turned back to Baumann. 'See that, Will? Ventura's ridin' Nimrod's hammer-head. Sure picked the right hoss, anyways, but he ain't likely to reach Plattville goin' at that lick!'

Baumann stepped across the threshold just in time to see the racing horseman disappear round the distant curve. 'I ain't so sure, Ollie. Mebbe he's got some Injun or Mex in him.'

'With yaller hair an' light eyes?'

'So?' Baumann shrugged. 'That don't mean a thing. What about the Valdés' for instance? But I didn't mean that exactly–' He broke off, frowning, thoughtfully tugged at his walrus moustache. 'They say a cavalryman can git so much out of a horse before it cracks; a good puncher can take it another twen'y miles; but an Injun'll push on another forty an' still not ride it into the ground!

'Aw! he ain't a fool, Ollie, soon's it starts blowin' he'll haul up. Come to think of it, wouldn't surprise me any if he *did* reach Plattville by first dark.'

'Wal,' the deputy grinned. 'I wouldn't take a bet on it, an' I'd shore admire to know what the fella's up to?'

161

'All he said was somethin' about makin' Holman pay. If he can do that, Ollie, I don't mind waitin' a while to see what it's all about.'

Ventura crouched in the saddle, exhilarated by the power and speed which this long-legged animal undoubtedly possessed to an astonishing degree. They must have covered between two and three miles already, yet not once had the buckskin put a foot wrong nor betrayed any signs of laboured breathing. He seemed to know what was wanted of him and was prepared to give it – too much so, perhaps, which likely was the reason Nimrod wouldn't hire him out as a rule. And it was not long before Ventura sensed this over-willingness on the buckskin's part, and realized that restraint over the first part of the journey might well pay off in the long run.

Shortly now he began easing the pace, finding it a not too easy task to check the buckskin's gallop and persuade the game animal to adopt a slower-paced but long-reaching lope.

Something of a tussle ensued, the buck-skin determined to maintain its own pace despite the now apparent blowing; Ventura, for his part, equally resolved to establish complete mastery and direction without re-course to any of the usual vicious tactics.

Gradually the steady pressure on the bit began to have its effect. Not only did the horse feel and sense the latent strength behind that steady pulling; he became growingly aware of his rider as a distinctive personality, in the inexplicable way of so many of the more domesticated animals. It has long been said that a good bronc-buster will breath into the horse's nostrils, thus establishing *una simpatia* – a sympathy which defies explanation or analysis. Maybe Ventura had done a similar thing, and the buckskin was playing a game, one which he was at length willing to quit.

Ventura felt the rhythm break and change under him even as the wind's force lessened on his face and body with the slower gait. The sweat trickled down the line of his jaw, channelling a series of furrows in the mask of alkali dust.

He drew rein, pulling the buckskin over to the shade of a cottonwood and judged the time as around three-thirty, the distance maybe seven miles. He waited out the space of ten-twelve minutes before springing to the saddle and reining back onto the twisting, dusty trail. And again it was un-necessary to spur – almost as though the ugly brute took relish in the exhibition of his own stamina and speed and responding now without resistance to the gently firm pressure of hand and knee.

At a half after five, Ventura pulled off the trail to a lone horse-ranch, the man eyeing him suspiciously at first, then relaxing sufficiently to produce a cup of hot java. Both rider and horse were streaming with sweat and trail-stained, yet neither seemed over-tired.

'You got a good hoss there, mister. But I guess you know that?'

Ventura nodded and cursed softly as the scalding coffee burned his tongue.

'Reckon he needs to be, *amigo*, to hold this pace clear through to Plattville. How far is it?'

''Bout eighteen miles.' He pointed across the low hills beyond the valley. 'You come in from Latigos, mebbe?'

'Sure.' Ventura showed the badge under his brush jacket. 'Urgent business in Plattville. Aim to make it before dark.' He squinted at the westering sun. 'I'd say it was 'tween five an' five-thirty, huh?'

The man nodded, regarded both horse and rider a moment. 'My name's Ned Smalley – hoss trader like you kin see. Light down, mister, an' let me rub down yore mount whiles you blow that java cool.'

There was something rather odd, yet at the same time likeable, about this sober-faced, bearded dealer, and with a faint, half-resigned smile, Ventura stepped from the saddle, still holding the mug of coffee.

164

He schooled himself to relax for a few minutes and ignore the quick passage of time. Blowing on the now cooling drink, he watched Smalley go about his chore with a methodical care, and suddenly it came home to Ventura that this man did not trade horses for a living only, but also because he loved them.

Too often, riders tended to regard their mounts merely as a means to an end, sometimes engaging in unnecessary cruelty. Unnecessary, because there was no call to flog a horse to death or rowel it unmercifully unless a man's life were actually at stake.

But Smalley was different, and the ugly hammer-head swung down and a bright eye rolled at Ventura almost knowingly as Smalley wiped foam from the mouth and stroked the soft muzzle.

'He'll be in a worse lather time you reach Plattville, mister; but that'll haveta do fer now, seein's yo're in such an all-fired hurry.'

Ventura planked the empty mug onto a low tree stump and shoved back his hat and found Smalley studying him again with a kind of flat curiosity.

'Thanks for the coffee, Smalley. As for the brute here, you done the slickest job in five minutes I ever seen.' He dug deep into his pants' pocket, came up with a gold piece and handed it to the horse-trader.

'I'll go get some change...'

'Never mind that. Mebbe I'll want you to do the same again tonight or tomorrow!'

'Sure. But twen'y bucks!'

Ventura swung up, and the falling sun shot oblique golden rays that touched his yellow hair and made it shine bright as the double eagle in Ned Smalley's hand.

'Hold it!' the man said quickly. 'Yore name wouldn't be Ventura, would it? Seems like I heerd you put the Injun sign on Diamond-back Smith way back, an' only the other day one o' Butler's desperadoes!'

'How you figure all this, Smalley?' Ventura was quietly watchful.

'Only this mawnin' a rider comes by, hoss lathered...' His shoulders lifted. 'Guess mebbe it ain't so unusual, but they wasn't no Injuns about far as I could see, nothin' bad like that as might make a man sink his spurs in deep.'

'This hombre,' Ventura said. 'He'd bin using his horse like that?'

The other nodded. 'Didn't care much for his looks even at fust. Started in talkin' 'bout places around: San Pablo, Plata, Latigos. Tell you the truth, mister, I found myself answerin' questions...'

'What kinda questions?'

'He asked if I'd ever heard of a bounty hunter name o' Ventura, and when I said yes, I had, he asked me to describe you. Wal, natcherally I couldn't. I said, "Lookit, mister, sure I've heerd of the man, but I ain't ever seen him. Far as I know," I said, "he ain't ever travelled this road".'

'So he was interested in me?' Ventura nodded. 'Sure, you guessed right first time, Smalley.'

'Wasn't so much a case o' guessin' once you shoved back that hat. But I reckon this hombre wan'ed to make plumb certain I was tellin' the truth. So he kinda alters his play an' says you an' him was pardners one time, that he'd heard of a man like you was in these parts; slim build but plen'y strong; dark complexion, blond hair, weight around one hun'ed an' sixty.'

'Quite a description,' Ventura murmured, 'which he'd obviously bin given by someone else. I guess, though, he didn't leave *his* name?'

The horse trader shook his head. 'Kinda evasive about himself he was, but I kin shore describe him for you, Mr Ventura, so's you'll know quick enough if you ever meet up with him...'

Scarcely a mile down the trail, the lights of Plattville glowed faintly in the misty approach of early night. And, incredible as it seemed even to Ventura himself, the ride had been accomplished in a little under five hours without a change of mount.

But both horse and rider presented a sorry

spectacle now, as wearily Ventura slid from leather, grasping the reins, and doggedly leading the jaded and limping animal along the trail to town.

With the stout-hearted buckskin being cared for at Taylor's Livery & Feed Barn, Ventura allowed himself a quick drink before heading out for the telegraph office located a short distance outside the town.

He rode a rented pony, and having obtained directions from the hostler, lost no time in reaching the spur track, loading pens and buildings of this small yet growing shipping point.

Some of the pens were full of bawling, restless steers waiting for tomorrow's dawn to be loaded into the waiting cars. A few cowpunchers drifted or lounged nearby, keeping an eye out for their stock, talking with buyers or their representatives, and doubtless impatient for their reliefs to show up on account trail-driving and night-hawking was such hell-fire thirsty work.

Here and there naphtha flares illumined the darkness, and from a rude shack belonging to the Longbough Cattle Syndicate, lamplight flared from windows and doorway, intensifying further the contrasts between brightness and deep shadow.

Ventura angled across to the telegraph office, tied his horse to a rack and tromped inside.

A shirt-sleeved clerk, wearing a green eye-shade, lifted his tired gaze, eyes squinted against the smoke wreathing upwards from the quirly pasted to his lower lip.

'Where can I find the telegraph operator?' The clerk jerked a thumb over his shoulder. 'Back in there, mister, but if you're figgerin' on sendin' a wire, better come back in a week's time.'

'Sure,' Ventura nodded, pushed open the wicket gate and stepped through to the door facing him. He could hear the tapping of the instrument's key through the flimsy panelling, and without knocking pushed open the door.

At a bench-like desk, a sheaf of papers at his left hand, the operator sat crouched over his instrument, tap-tapping with the key as he held a pencil to each word in turn on the written message before him.

Once he glanced up, pointed to a stack of blank forms, and continued sending out his Morse signals without a pause.

By the time he had tapped out two more messages, Ventura was through, and passed the pink sheet across to the bespectacled operator.

'Unlikely to go fer some time, mister, maybe a day or so. Line's busier now than–'

'The code word to clear the line is Chicago Flyer,' Ventura said quietly. 'Make it fast, hombre.'

The man's eyebrows popped up as he glared at his visitor and then quickly transferred his gaze to the neatly pencilled message. It read:

Major Frank Arlen, Palace Avenue, Santa Fe.

Request your permission force Richard Holbrook, alias Roy Holman, replace cattle herd recently destroyed on his orders by suggesting new evidence available on Holbrook-Jackson killing. This is urgent personal matter. Fresh lead on Flare. Will write in detail and await your immediate answer. Signed Ventura.

'Bigosh!' Behind the telegraph man's spectacles his eyes were circles of shocked surprise as he finished reading. His glance swivelled to the clock on the wall. 'I – I'm supposed to give it another ten minutes for incomin' stuff, then start transmitting again. As it is, I reckon we'd best get started clearing the line.'

Ventura nodded. 'Make sure a reliable man is standing by to hand this wire to Major Arlen personally. The messenger'll be paid for his trouble.'

'Yessir!' The operator sure wasted little time, and watching the way he went to work and listening to the rapid-fire buzzing of the Morse key, Ventura had to admire the manner in which the business was handled. Exactly seventeen minutes later the sweating official swung triumphantly round in his chair. 'Your message is now through to

Santa Fe, Mr Ventura– Just a minute...' He whirled again as the instrument sprang to life with a call signal. In a moment or two he looked up and grinned. 'Carradine, our man at Santa Fe, jest called back. He's fixin' to get a fellow out to Palace Avenue *pronto,* but it might be a few hours before we can receive a reply. There's a few other priorities!'

Ventura nodded and indicated the cot against the wall. 'All right for me to catch a little sleep?'

'Well – it's strictly against the rules, Mr Ventura...' His voice trailed away as the bounty hunter laid an eagle on the desk and without further word pulled off the dusty boots and stretched himself full length on the blankets. In five seconds flat he was sleeping as deeply as a child.

Yet some four hours later he came awake on the instant his name was called.

'Your reply, Mr Ventura,' the operator grinned. 'Not bad going, considering they had quite a job finding Major Arlen.'

Ventura's eyes lifted to the clock. The time was near eleven-thirty.

'It's still good going.' He took the paper on which the major's brief reply had been written, glanced at it smilingly, and thrust it into an inside pocket.

'You keep copies of all messages sent out?'

'Sure.' The man indicated a ledger-type book open on the desk. 'Most often I copy

171

it down left-handed while I'm tapping. Kinda saves time that way. But all priorities are treated as confidential and recorded in a special book.'

'What about my original form?'

'Destroyed as soon as the message has been sent out and copied down.'

Ventura pulled on his boots, stepped across and laid another eagle on the desk. 'Where's the best place to eat?'

'You cain't beat Ma Ketchley's, Mr Ventura, four blocks along on Main from here,' the operator grinned. 'Likely she's still open.'

'Gracias,' Ventura murmured and stepped quietly out into the night...

A pity to have to leave the buckskin behind, but there had been no alternative. Strong and willing as the horse was, it would not be fully recovered for several days. Meanwhile, the long-legged roan which Taylor had swapped him was maintaining a steady, mile-eating lope through the night. It needed more frequent resting, and lacked the hammer-head's phenomenal speed, yet it was still horse-flesh at its best and Ventura handled it accordingly, taking a sight longer over the return journey, despite the two pressing appointments he had lined up for Valdés and Holman.

In the small hours Smalley opened up to Ventura's insistent rapping with an understandable reluctance. He kept well to one side of the door, careful not to make a target of himself for some horse-thief's gun. Dull lamplight gleamed softly on the blue-black Colt's pistol outthrust from the shadows.

'This is Ventura!'

Smalley made quite certain before inviting his caller in. Afterwards, he put fresh coffee on the stove, set a plate of crackers and cream cheese before the dust-covered rider, and reached for a pipe and tobacco.

'You ain't come back on the buckskin, an' you got some ways to go yet. You want a fresh mount?'

Ventura shook his head. 'A long-legged roan from Taylor's. He'll make it, Smalley, if he's not pushed too hard.'

The man nodded, bent over the coffee pot and peered inside. 'Ain't properly warmed yet...'

Outside, a horse nickered shrilly, almost on the same moment that the door crashed open with shocking violence.

'*Ventura!*'

The single name leaped from the stranger's throat as he stood framed in the doorway, left hand braced against the door's recoil, right arm extended straight at Ventura, and in the hand a levelled Navy Colt.

And once again, as when he had taken Hank Dillis, the bounty hunter moved like chain lightning, brain and instinct together furnishing him with the sure certainty that

173

this in fact was the man Smalley had described only last night. This same black-hatted stranger in the creased homespun suit who had for no good reason bloodied his horse with cruel spurs and had sought information concerning Ventura.

Right on top of that ringing challenge, it seemed, came Smalley's frantic shout: *'That's the man–!'* Yet, quick as he was, his warning words were drowned in the close-in roar of guns and the vicious whine of lead...

CHAPTER X

'KEEP RIDIN', FERRIS!'

At the moment of action, Ventura had catapulted from his place at the table, sending his chair crashing backwards. But even as he drew and fired, pain burned his left leg high up on the thigh, and he thumbed back the gun-hammer a second time and steadied himself and saw his adversary's gun slide from fingers now too slack to grip.

The man was still in a half-crouched position, but the savage purpose had drained from him with the gush of blood from his arm.

174

'D – don't shoot again, Ventura! Don't kill me! I…'

Slowly Ventura sheathed his gun as Ned Smalley turned the lamp higher with a none-too-steady hand and retrieved his own gun from the shelf where he had laid it previously. But there was no need to cover or threaten the wounded man now. He was swaying a little as he strove to stem the flow of blood from his upper arm.

Anger rode Ventura as he stepped forward and scooped up the fallen Navy Colt. Yet deep down inside him was a trickle of relief as well. Sometimes there was no alternative to killing, like when Gil James had drawn and the bounty hunter had had to make very sure, coupling speed with marksmanship to the full stretch of his ability.

But here the set-up had been a mite different. If the black-hatted hombre had played his hand differently, maybe Ventura would not have had the opportunity to leap aside and simultaneously dive for his gun. Likely one man, if not two, would have been killed.

Ventura let go his breath in a juddering sigh. 'All right, mister. You can thank your lucky stars the bullet didn't go a few inches to your left. Sit down over here, where we can see you.'

'I don't get it,' Ned Smalley growled. 'The lousy so-an'-so musta bin layin' fer you

175

some place outside, but how did he know—'

'Never mind that. We'll question him later. Right now if his arm's not fixed he's gonna pass out!'

A kettle of water stood atop the stove with the coffee pot, and shortly Ventura had the ugly flesh wound bathed and cleansed. The man's eyes were closed and sweat ran down his putty-coloured face; his breathing was rapid, and underneath the now opened shirt, his chest rose and fell sharply.

'You got some whisky, Ned?'

'Sure. I'll get it.' Smalley pondered a moment, trying to figure something out, and then, with a faint shrug, moved across to the cupboard and returned with a bottle.

'All right!' Ventura said later. 'First off, what's your name?'

The horse-dealer poured hot coffee into three mugs set out on the table. 'What about your own wound?' He pointed to the bullet-burn over the pants' pocket and the small dark stain surrounding, and Ventura unbuckled his belts, folding down the top of his trousers to reveal a small dark patch on the pale flesh of his skin. The grimness in his face was slowly receding.

'No more'n a scratch, Ned. Guess I had forgotten about it, dam' near.' He reached for the whisky bottle, dabbed some spirit onto the graze and managed to tie his handkerchief round for protection.

'I – I reckon I got to thank you – Ventura. You – you'd 'a' bin within yore rights to finish me…' The gunman raised pale green eyes in which swam both perplexity and pain. 'Or mebbe I got it wrong! Mebbe yo're figgerin' on…'

'Only if you don't come clean, mister, an' get on with the story! What's your name? Who sicced you on me? What's behind it all? You better talk an' talk fast, dam' you…'

'Sure! Take it easy, will you? I'm willin' to talk – if I kin forgit this stinkin' pain a moment! Name's Bob Ferris an' I'm – I was tied in with – with Torch Butler's crowd!'

'Torch Butler! Mebbe we're getting somewhere!' Ventura breathed softly. He studied Ferris intently; the dark roan hair wet now and limp with sweat; the reddish-gold whiskers and sea-green eyes. Features rugged and normally florid; build, chunky and heavy, and height not above five and a half feet.

'Look, mister…!' Ferris licked his dry lips and took a quick gulp of coffee. 'I – I ain't figgerin' on sellin' out Torch an' the boys, if that's what yo're thinkin'! I ain't tellin' where they are, not you or the law! But you an' me together – that's different! Like I said, you could 'a' finished the job jest now. Most fellas fast as you was wouldn't 'a' wasted whisky an' – an' pity on the hombre as laid fer 'em.' He turned his gaze on the

177

listening horse-trader. 'Lucky fer me you didn't decide to use that cannon!'

'Mebbe I should 'a' done so when you fust showed up with yore spurs drippin' blood,' Ned Smalley snarled. 'I ain't got no time for yellow-bellied killers like you! You—'

'Hold it, Ned!' Ventura turned to the wounded man. 'Tell me why Torch Butler wants me out of the way! I'm not asking where he is, but—'

'Sure, sure. I'm tellin' you, Ventura. It was on account St–Wal, they heard about Hank Dillis. Yeah! Both Torch an' Jim Butler got to figgerin' you was too dangerous, Ventura, for their peace o' mind.'

'So! They called you up, gave you my description an' mebbe a nice little bonus, an' told you to take care of me any way you wanted, just so long as you did a clean job!'

Surprise flickered a moment in Bob Ferris' watery eyes. 'You sound like you know 'em—?'

'Mebbe! Mebbe it's just this particular breed I know. Well, Ferris—' Ventura picked up the heavy Navy Colt, ejected the spent shell and the five live ones, and sat hefting the gun, gazing at the man speculatively. It was then that Ferris seemed to catch his first glimpse of the deputy's star momentarily visible under Ventura's brush jacket.

'Bigawd! They didn't tell me you was a *lawman!* They all got you figgered as a scalp-hunter! Say – this is a trick then! You ain't gonna let me go! Yo're fixin' to turn me in...!' His voice ascended the scale until it cracked. His breathing again became laboured and in the lamplight his face glistened wetly.

'Listen, Ferris!' There was a quality in Ventura's voice not heard before. 'Mebbe I'm a fool to even consider lettin' you go.' He rolled and lit a quirly and drank down his coffee, and both the others sat there in a waiting silence.

'Once a man starts in killing, either for reward or merely to satisfy some strange urge, then it starts gettin' a habit. Likely he earns for himself a reputation an' another fool comes along and braces him just to prove he can shoot straighter and faster! Sure, mebbe, it'll be a long time yet before men have no need to wear guns; just so long as hombres like you, Ferris, are willing to do the bidding of murderers and thieves like the Butlers!' He pulled open the brush jacket to reveal the law badge completely. 'I'm not a paid deputy employed by San Pablo County officials; just sworn in for a special job, is all. That's one reason why I aim to make my own decisions on this, Ferris.

'But you take my advice and ride clear of men like Ketchum and the Butlers. Sooner or later, just as surely as the smaller fry are bein' caught, so will the big fish.'

'So help me! I ain't fixin' to ride back to Torch, mister! Like as not I'd be signin' my own death certificate! But...' Again Bob Ferris regarded the other in perplexity. 'I cain't figger why–'

'I guess you wouldn't. But I recall a small town down along the Border and a saloon called The Silver Spurs. 'Twas mebbe fourteen-fifteen years back an' a younker got himself into a rigged poker game – the usual thing. They let him win a packet, then started to clean up. The kid was sharp enough to spot the trick and quick enough to get his gun out first!'

Ferris' eyes were wide open and bright, gaze clinging to Ventura's face. He shifted the injured arm a little and seemed almost to forget the pain.

'You know who I'm talkin' about now, Ferris, though that wasn't your name in those days. Sure! It took me quite a while to recognize you, but by the time Ned and me had fixed your arm I was more than halfway sure.'

'Mebbe this *is* my lucky day, after all,' Ferris croaked. 'Thar ain't many hombres with a mem'ry as long as that, an' *I* don't recollect–'

Ventura shook his head. 'I guess you had no call to, and it doesn't matter. The point was, those Federal troops and newly-elected

Peace Officers were out to show how tough they were. Kids like you, Ferris, were easy meat, even though you *did* shoot in self-defence.'

'That's it, Ventura! Bigawd, you shore have got the picture to rights! But I lit out; heard they was after me fer murder...'

'That tinhorn chiseller *didn't* die, Ferris, though he came dam' near to it. But those hombres runnin' the town couldn't forget the war was over, and it was they and their kind as sent many a kid ridin' a trail he couldn't quit!'

'By hickory!' Smalley grunted, 'if this don't beat all get-out!'

Ventura stood up, thumbs hooked into his gun-belt. 'I'm not askin' what you've done since that day long ago, Ferris, but so far as I know, there's no reward notices bin posted for you, not around this Territory anyway, which likely means you haven't bin tied with Butler for very long!'

'That's true; only a few months, is all. I bin all over, Ventura, clear to the Canady border, rustlin', hold-ups, sometimes even an' honest job or two. Then I came south again, after many years. I killed a man an' wounded another...' He scowled, gestured with his good arm. 'The details don't matter an' I ain't makin' excuses. Mebbe they got a right to hang me an' there'd be no kicks comin'. Still an' all, if yo're figgerin' to give

181

me a break, all this you told me makes things kinda different. You wanta know who told Torch about you–'

'It was Steve Crow, wasn't it?'

The desperado stared, his be-whiskered jaw sagging wide.

'Like you said awhile back, Ferris, details don't matter. I had Crow figured for the part, but I wasn't dead sure. Now I am!

'But there's something more important that the law would like to know right now.'

'You mean the hideout?'

Ventura nodded, handed the empty Colt's pistol across, and watched as Ferris painfully and laboriously eased it into the scabbard with his left hand. He fought the spasm of pain in silence, mouth now ironed into a hard line of resistance. Yet, when his glance lifted, he achieved a thin, twisted smile.

'Guess I'll haveta learn me a left-handed cross-draw now!'

'You ride clear of coyotes, mebbe you won't find the need.'

Ferris nodded. 'Gimme a pencil an' paper.'

Ventura produced a stub of pencil and an old, unused envelope and laid them on the table. With a little help, the ex-member of Torch Butler's gang produced a reasonably accurate sketch-map, pin-pointing the bluffs and wooded slopes that circled the hideout.

'A sheep-farm, huh?'

Ferris nodded, explaining in terse sentences the whole layout and what he knew concerning the men there.

'Mebbe they'll be figgerin' I sold 'em,' he husked. 'Mebbe they'll say I turned yaller an' fixed to save my own neck. Wal, the hell with what them coyotes think! I see it different now an' that's the way it's gonna be, if I get the chance...'

'You'll have to clear out of this county *pronto*, for obvious reasons, and that means ridin' just as you are.'

'I'll make out,' the man gritted. 'There's a fella I worked with fer a spell in Torrance, runs a small spread. Mebbe we clapped an iron on a few mavericks now and again, but–'

'You won't get clear through to Torrance County without seeing a doctor.'

'I kin try. You an' Smalley fixed it real good. Sure it hurts like hell, but it ain't bleedin' now, I reckon.'

Ventura shook his head, fished into a pocket for more paper and wrote something in pencil. He handed the sheet to Ferris. 'This is the name and address of a medico in Albuquerque. He'll make sure the wound's free of poison; mebbe let you rest up for a few days. Tell him I sent you.'

'Why, I – I–'

Ned Smalley could scarcely believe his own eyes at sight of this rough-and-tumble character almost overcome by Ventura's proferred help.

'Wal,' the horse-trader grunted, climbing to his feet. 'That bein' the case, I guess the least I kin do is rustle you up some grub fer yore saddle-pouches...'

Dawn was still little more than pale promise in the east, and in the yard Bob Ferris sat astride his horse. A new Bob Ferris whose face was turned towards the south-east, towards the future.

'You got a clean sheet, so far as I know,' Ventura reminded him. 'Keep it that way. Head for Albuquerque, an' keep ridin', Ferris!'

When Ventura rode into Latigos some time after nine o'clock he was feeling too dead beat to think about anything beyond sleep.

He left the exhausted roan at the livery, sparing Nimrod only a brief explanation before heading straight back to the Bosque House.

Timothy, the day clerk, handed over the key, and immediately Ventura entered his room he locked the door, threw himself onto the bed and was asleep in seconds...

He had left word to be called at two o'clock, and right on the stroke a coloured boy hammered on the door and showed the still travel-stained bounty hunter to the bathroom.

Presently, feeling considerably refreshed, he descended to the dining-room and ordered a double portion of steak and fried potatoes. While waiting, he rolled a quirly and walked through to the hotel lobby and across to the desk.

He laid out some coins in front of the clerk. 'Tim, get a message over to the marshal, will you? Tell him I'm back and could he see me for a moment in the dining-room!'

'Sure, Mr Ventura. Right away, sir!'

He returned to his table as Minnie smilingly set down a heaped-up plate of food.

'Like me to get you a nice cool beer, Mr Ventura?'

He smiled up at her and nodded, and Minnie hurried away, her day made bright. He was halfway through the meal when Baumann came through the draped opening, paused a second, and then tromped over, drawing up a chair.

'Wal, so you got back, huh? Hope you found the breakneck ride paid off?' There was an unmistakable note of sarcasm in Baumann's rhetorical question and Ventura grinned sympathetically.

'Reckon as a deputy I'm a kinda disappointment, eh, Will?' He speared a piece of meat onto the fork and chewed with obvious enjoyment.

'First man-sized meal I've had since

around eleven-thirty last night!'

'I shore am sorry about that, brother! Mebbe whoever employs you don't pay enough for you to eat regular!'

'So you figure I'm working for someone, huh?'

Baumann shrugged expressively. 'Could be. Likely I'll find out one o' these days.'

Ventura pushed his plate to one side as Minnie came over with a tray of apple pie and cream. He waited until the girl had withdrawn. 'I'm hoping it won't be too long before I can give you the whole set-up, Will. But first off, there's one-two things more I gotta find out.'

'What – who about? Is this anythin' to do with ridin' to Plattville an' sending a wire, mebbe?'

'No, not exactly. That was something more – huh – personal, I guess. But as a Peace Officer yourself, Will, you'll understand that a man's not always free to show his hand.'

'Sure. Mebbe that sheriff's star you showed me the other days mean's somethin' more'n a keepsake yo're totin' around. But if this business concerns the Butler boys or anythin' like that, then I'd shore admire to be put in the picture!'

'As a matter of fact, I'll be counting on your help, Marshal, when the time comes. Right now I'm going to pay Arrow a visit.'

The home buildings on Holman's spread reflected quite some of their owner's personality. They were big and rambling, and almost crude in appearance, and patently built strictly for utilitarian purposes.

Nothing here but the basic essentials, Ventura considered, as he kneed the steeldust across the yard and let his gaze sweep over barns, corrals and bunkhouse.

Sun, wind and rain had long since stripped paint from most of the woodwork, though some attempt had been made apparently to maintain the ranch-house itself in slightly more attractive fashion.

A covered veranda on which stood a scattering of chairs faced onto the ill-kept yard, and here both furniture and veranda itself betrayed evidence of recent freshening coats of white paint.

In the corral yonder a string of cow ponies moved, heads lifted inquisitively, ears pricked forward. Beyond the barns and stables a windmill's sails showed grey against the white-clouded blue of the sky, and from somewhere nearby the strident blows of a blacksmith's hammer rang in Ventura's ears.

Without any warning a man appeared from the region of the bunkhouse and started walking slowly forward, eyes fixed unswervingly on the man astride the steeldust.

Although he was obviously an Arrow hand, and on his home ground, he wore a shell-belt and carried a black-handled gun in the tied-down holster. Maybe James was dead, but it looked like he had at least one successor.

Ten yards off he hauled up and stood with bowed legs apart, thumbs hooked loosely into his belt.

'If yo're Ventura, mister,' he said with cold malevolence, 'you shore got one helluva goddam nerve!'

'I don't recollect leavin' my card,' Ventura said softly.

The puncher spat with calculated deliberation. 'We all heard what Gil's killer looked like, mister. Ain't likely they's two of you around these parts. Reckon that must make you Ventura.'

'Where's Holman?'

'You ain't finished with me yet, mister gunslick—'

'Hake!'

The man's tense muscles slowly relaxed. For a long moment he continued gazing into Ventura's face as though loath to miss any precious detail. Then he turned his head towards the house.

'All right, Hake!' Holman bellowed, and waved his arm in an impatient gesture that could have meant anything or nothing.

'Wanta talk with you, Holman.' Ventura

scarcely raised his voice, and without invitation gigged his mount over to the house porch, and all the time he felt the trickle of icy water down his back, wondering about the gun-crazy Hake behind him. He heard the man's boots crunch on gravel and reined the steel-dust quickly so that he had both Arrow men within his range of vision.

There was an expression on Roy Holman's huge, florid face at once angry yet viciously cunning.

'So you wanta see me, huh? Wal, Ventura, I cain't think of anythin' I wanta talk to *you* about, less'n it's to tell you a little story about a goddam fool, jest like you, who once figgered he was smart enough to brace me!'

'What happened?' Ventura asked softly. 'You get the gun-hungry James or Happy Hake here, to throw his body into a ravine?'

The silence beat down on the trio, each man feeling its heavy, breathless weight, each man, for one reason or another, remaining still, scarcely a nerve twitching.

'I reckon you ain't gonna live much longer, mister!' Hake's voice was so choked with bitter fury he was not far removed from incoherence.

Without seeming to move a muscle, Ventura allowed the brush jacket to open further.

'Take it easy, Hake!' Holman snarled.

'Dam' me if he ain't hidin' behind a tin-star. By God....!'

Now Ventura's voice cut through the words with the biting lash of a bull whip.

'Call your watch-dog off, Holman, else I'm gonna start somethin' you'll be sorry for! Somethin' that San Pablo or mebbe Santa Fe'll finish – if I can't!'

The Arrow owner's face turned from roan to putty-colour. For perhaps the first time he seemed to have lost just a fraction of his blustering and ruthless arrogance. Unhurriedly and with no suggestion of hostile movement, he lifted his left hand to finger the luxuriant longhorn moustache above his lips, and for an ice-cold moment Ventura wondered if it was a signal for Hake to take him.

But no one moved until Holman himself shifted his gaze and looked at his henchman.

'All right, Hake, saddle up the new paint an' teach it some cow-work!'

With dragging reluctance Hake moved away, hard, unforgiving stare pinned to this cool blond man who had, in some not quite understandable way, out-drawn and out-shot Gil.

He paused long enough to say his final piece, hurling the words at Ventura from a distance of thirty yards or more. *Some other time, mister!* he promised, and turned towards the pole corral.

In a moment Ventura had unshipped and climbed the porch steps, Holman watching and taking no more trouble to hide his hatred than had Hake.

'Better make it fast,' he said. 'I'm a pretty busy man, an' besides which, I couldn't guarantee hauling the rest o' the crew off yore back, should they ride in!'

'Listen, Holman, and get this! Your gun-crazy Hake doesn't scare me, because I've met the breed plen'y times before. You better tell him, too, that if he lays a hand on that gun he's liable to get the same treatment as James!'

Ventura stood with his back against the house-front, arms loosely folded across his chest, his glance flickering over the Arrow owner and across the wide expanse of yard beyond.

'Mebbe you ain't sized up Hake quite right, mister. Nor me neither! By the time I've finished tellin' the legislature that one o' their members has bin threatened by a cheap, bounty-huntin' gunfighter–'

'You won't tell them any such thing,' Ventura said softly. 'Not if you're as smart as I've bin informed. Right now I got news from Santa Fe that new evidence has bin dug up on the Jackson killing! Remember Cinch Jackson, Holman, back in Newton? Remember how you got off and cleaned up nicely in the process? Remember–?'

'How do *you* know about what happened back there in Kansas?' Holman whispered hoarsely. 'An' what's it gotta do with anyone down here in *this* Territory? The case was closed, an' lawmen don't–' He checked suddenly as the thought came to him and with it, the beginnings of an understanding.

'So,' he nodded, 'yo're a lawman, mister, is that it? Not jest Baumann's hired help, but…' Again he paused, vaguely conscious of the fact that this man was leading him on to talk. He moved over to where Ventura lounged, the veranda boards creaking under his great weight; that, and the soft scrape of his custom-made boots, the only sounds in the drawn-out silence.

CHAPTER XI

A HERD FOR A HERD

'All right, Ventura! Mebbe you *could* stir up enough mud to make it – huh – kinda awkward. But it might be a good idea if you was to explain a few things! Such as, f'r instance, accusin' innocent citizens of killin' and throwin'…'

'I didn't *accuse* you, Holman! I just

naturally asked a question in that instance.' He lifted his shoulders. 'Don't faze yourself about the Fletcher boys, even if they were a pair o' double-crossin' coyotes.'

'You couldn't prove a dam' thing about them riders, hombre; neither you nor anyone else, an' you know it!'

'Mebbe you're right about that.' Ventura spoke as though the Fletcher killings no longer interested him. 'But you're sure gonna pay to keep this new evidence out of the newspapers, out of the public eye...'

Understanding dawned in Holman's dark eyes, and was as quickly followed by a sudden apprehension. But when he answered, it was in a louder voice with more than a little return of the old brashness.

'I don't pretend to know what you got on me – or what you *figger* you got, mister, but I do know you'd have one helluva time provin' anythin' in a court o' law. I come a long way since those days back in Kansas, an' no two-bit Pinkerton man *or* Federal Officer's gonna interfere now. And I'll tell you this much, you lousy, gun-totin' bustard, I got friends on the assembly at Santa Fe: judges, industrial leaders, an' some o' the best lawyers in the Territory. Another thing, hombre. They's two ways o' dealin' with cases like this. One's bringin' it out in the open, even if it means fixin' a jury. The other's– Wal, I guess mebbe yo're smart enough to figger that one for yoreself!'

'Quite a speech!' Ventura unfolded his arms and hooked thumbs loosely into his bun-belt. 'But like so many o' them politicin' harangues, full of hot air.' He eyed Holman coldly, and pushed away from the wall, forcing the other to step back a pace. A small thing, yet not without its effect on a roughshod bully.

'Now, let's get to the point, Mr Rich Holbrook. Like I said, mebbe you *could* fix things, but there's always the doubt, and for sure there'd be plen'y scandal, not to mention expense! Just how much you reckon it'd set you back to fix a specially subpoenaed court?' He shook his head. 'More thousands than you'd care to reckon up, Holman! As for the other alternative you got in mind, I sure don't advise that, on account there's a sealed letter in Santa Fe – already for openin' if I don't show up by a certain date. Your name's in it, mister, and this'd be the one bushwhackin' you wouldn't get away with! See what I mean?

'No, Holman. You'll do like I say on account it's not only safer – but cheaper!'

The Arrow owner ran the tip of his tongue over dry lips, glancing quickly around him.

'How much?'

'Exactly three hundred an' thirty head of prime beef!'

Holman stared, not even attempting to

194

mask his surprise. For a full minute he made no reply, his brain racing, trying hard to figure the angles. Once his glance drifted over towards the outbuildings, but he read the danger in Ventura's frosty eyes and discarded the desperate thought.

'What else?' he snarled. 'A gold poke tied to each pair o' horns?'

'Nothin' else. Just three hundred an' thirty head is all, delivered to Starcross together with a proper bill of sale! You didn't figure to get off so light, did you?'

'Are you crazy or somethin'? What the hell is all this about? Why Starcross, an' where do *you* collect – or are you askin' me to believe–' Abruptly Holman pulled up in mid-sentence. *'Why three hun'ed an' thirty steers, Ventura?'* he demanded in an anger-choked whisper.

The bounty hunter smiled thinly and withdrew tobacco sack and papers. He rolled a quirly, his eyes never long removed from the scene in front of him. He took his time over lighting the cigarette, knowing that such studied trivialities had their irritating effect on a man as brashly impetuous as this one.

'A herd for a herd,' he answered slowly. 'Three hundred and twen'y five was the number of Starcross cattle the Fletcher boys fed on locoweed, an' I figure another five for interest, and likely that's rating it low...'

'Why, you—'

'Shut up, Holman! You've had your say, an' now I'm having mine. Let's not dicker over words like "proof" or "evidence". We both know you planted those Fletcher rats at Starcross to kill the trail herd scheduled for Fort Frazer.'

'By God! You know so much, hombre, then tell me why I'd do a thing like that an' mebbe risk my whole future, my neck...?'

'There wasn't so much risk. Only trouble was the Fletcher brothers themselves when they started gettin' too ambitious. Mebbe they wanted a bigger slice – *quién sabe?*' He shrugged. 'That was when you sicced James and the boys onto them, a convenient excuse to make sure they'd never talk!

'As for the reason, Holman, that's somethin' else we both understand, isn't it?'

'You know more'n is healthy fer anyone!' the big man whispered, and turned away, staring out over the vast yard, half-wishing that dusk were here and the crew would ride in and, at a signal, cut this trouble-shooter to ribbons and to hell with the risk!

But inwardly, Roy Holman knew it would be plain suicide to attempt such a thing, when more than likely Baumann, if not others in town, knew where this tin-horn deputy had come today. And there was this letter at Santa Fe. It could be a bluff, but Ventura had taken enough tricks already to prove he held dam' near a full-house. No, it would be crazy to call against him right now. Later, perhaps, away from the ranch, Hake or Plummer would be only too willing to even the score!

He heard Ventura move behind him and then that hateful voice reached out, cold and deadly like the first deep frost of winter.

'By tomorrow, Roy, an' no loose ends!'

Holman faced around, and something which had been vaguely puzzling now became clear. Lawman, politician, trader, storekeeper, outlaw – it didn't matter a dam'. Every man had his price and every man was eager to take his cut. With Ventura it was just the same, except this man's percentage was not dollars alone nor even stock; it was *Judith Valdés herself and the rich grazing lands of Starcross!* The same prize he himself was aiming for! Now the pattern was clear, or understandable at least, and he felt a resurgence of his confidence and strength and saw a way he might use Ventura's plan to his own advantage.

'All right! Suppose we play it yore way! What guarantee 've I got yo're not fixin' a double-cross after them steers are delivered? What about this letter? Looks to me like you ain't the only one in this business. Likely you got a boss...'

'More a partner than a boss. But just so long as those cattle are turned over to Starcross, you got my word that the evidence and the letter'll be destroyed!'

'Your word?' Holman's dark eyes snapped wide for a moment and then he laughed, almost completely his old bombastic self. He thought: *This hombre is just the kinda fool who would keep his word whatever it cost!*

The moment Ventura had ridden clear of the yard, Holman pounded down the veranda steps and across to the corrals. But Hake was ready and waiting.

'Saddle up an' trail him, Hake! I wanta know if he's headin' out fer Starcross or returnin' to town!'

Hake's bitter gaze stayed on the slowly diminishing shape of horse and rider. 'I kin make a clean job, Roy, right away from here, you jest say the word!'

Holman's big hand rested on the man's gun-arm for a moment in tacit warning. 'Not this time, Hake. They'll know he's bin out here an' we'd never get away with it. Later on, mebbe, we'll have the chance. I gotta idea we might kill the two birds at one go, both him an' Santeely... Now listen, Hake, here's what you gotta do, an' no slip-ups, see?

'Like I said, find out which way he's headin' an' keep on his trail till you can be dam' certain. If he makes fer town, don't stop him; jest ride back here fast. But if he decides to light out fer Starcross, stick close,

198

an' soon's he's off Arrow range, bust his shoulder with a Winchester slug. You got that?'

'Sure. But how'd you know I won't drop the slug lower, in his goddam heart, or bust his neck?'

Holman laughed. 'First because I tell you; second because Hake Murray can place a shot where he wants, and third, on account it's worth an extra hundred bucks! Get movin', Hake!'

The gunman indicated a pony standing ground-hitched in a patch of evening shade. 'Already saddled, Roy.' He walked across and caught up the reins, climbing leisurely into the hull, and with a curt nod trotted his mount away from the home buildings.

Holman's quick eye looked for and found the rifle in its saddle-boot and he nodded approval. Hake was in many ways even better than James had been, just so long as he kept a curb chain on his vicious hatred.

Loeson, the ex-bronc-peeler, was squatting against a grain bin when Holman roused him.

'Saddle the black for me, Fred, an' be dam' quick about it!'

Loeson got up, going about his task with such painful slowness that the Arrow owner swung impatiently on his heel and crossed over to the house, emerging shortly hat in hand and with a lighted cigar clenched between his big yellow teeth. Loeson knew too much to give him his time, Holman reflected, and the fool wasn't worth killing anyway.

It was all of twenty minutes before he was able to ride through the yard, yet there was nothing he could do until Hake returned. He rode on, eventually pulling into the shade of an overhang, and remained in the saddle, alternately chewing and puffing at the expensive cigar, his florid face set in scowling lines of thought. Daylight began to roll away towards the first creeping mists of dusk, and impatience crawled over the man at this enforced activity.

He found himself listening for the sound of a distant shot, doubting for a moment the wisdom of entrusting Hake with this particular chore. Maybe he should have explained that all he wanted right now was to stop Ventura riding to Starcross. Possibly the bounty hunter, or whatever he was, would figure tomorrow morning was soon enough to warn Valdés and Summers that an Arrow herd was arriving.

As to how Ventura might explain the whole thing to Judith and Esteban, Roy Holman had already figured that angle. It all rather hung on whether the hombre kept his promise, and to Holman he still seemed like the kind of dumb fool to do just that thing. As a matter of fact, this little scheme might very well not work at all, and in any case, sooner or later details were likely to emerge that would show Holman as a liar and worse.

Yet the Arrow owner considered it was worth a try and might even produce a useful breathing space. He had gambled on less certain things even than this before now, and hit the jackpot.

The black's ears twitched forward and then Holman heard the distant pound of hooves. Shortly, a rider showed sky-lined for a few seconds atop a ridge before plunging down the grassy slope to continue on at full stretch. It was Hake all right, and Holman felt a twinge of relief that apparently no attack on Ventura had been necessary. When the right time came it would be something far more fatal than a carefully placed slug in the shoulder!

Holman moved out from the tree's cast shadow as Murray quickly reduced the distance between them. In a little while he was pulling the wet pony back on its haunches in a sliding stop alongside the waiting Arrow owner.

Hake wiped sweat from his leather face and allowed himself two or three deep breaths before giving his news.

'Figgered at first he was gonna head fer Starcross like you said he might. He reined in at Mustang Gap all right, but jest smoked a quirly is all, before hittin' the trail to town!'

'He kept straight on, Hake?'

'Sure. But I followed a ways, keepin' outa sight, then, to make sure, I climbed a high knoll an' watched from the brush. He ain't headin' anywheres right now 'ceptin' Latigos, Roy.'

'Right. Like I promised, you'll get yore chance, Hake, I ain't got much doubt. Now, when the boys come in, tell Larry I'm over to Starcross and will be back around eight, I guess. I shall wanta see you both then, *sabe?*'

Murray nodded, tugged his hat down and touched spurt to his mount, and as he rode off, Roy Holman pointed the black gelding towards the cut-offs quartering on Starcross.

Ventura finished writing the letter, re-read it through and made a couple of small alterations. He signed his name, folded the paper and slipped it inside the addressed envelope. There lay one of the reasons he had decided against calling on Judith this evening. He had promised Frank Arlen a written report on Torch Butler, or Flare as he had referred to him, and today the bi-weekly Plattville coach pulled out at six.

The other important thing was his 'appointment' with Esteban Valdés, now long overdue. He only hoped that Santeely had been able to handle his end of the business. Likely enough by this time Mr Steve Crow was feeling plenty sore!

Ventura stepped from the Bosque House and crossed to the rack where he had left the steel-dust tied. He still had to play this close to his vest as far as everyone here was concerned, even including Will Baumann, and he took care now to avoid the marshal's office. He stopped off at the Express office just long enough to entrust his letter to Billy Sharpless, and once again hauled himself into leather and headed out of town, this time for Santeely's isolated cabin on the Jarvis strip.

Twilight had quickly given way to early night, and across the darkening sky wispy clouds drifted like thinning gunsmoke before a myriad of tiny lights.

Ventura took the route along which he and Santeely had returned to town two nights back with the body of Gil James. At times the going was rougher and the upward climb steeper than the trails he had ridden when following the tracks of Dulcie Randell's buckboard. But it saved a few miles, and he was feeling the deep weariness, mental as well as physical, of so many near-continuous hours in the saddle.

A light gleamed out of the darkness ahead, and as he came through the brush, skirting the sweep of blackly silhouetted junipers, he reined in, listening, and searched the night shadows with watchful care.

Satisfied, he put the steel-dust to the yard and hailed the house, and knew a mild relief when Mike Santeely called back an answer through the open door.

Ventura came on and saw then that the nester was taking no chances. Away from the light he stood, with a shot-gun in his hands.

'It's okay, Ventura.' Santeely smiled half apologetically. 'Just wanted to make certain. Light down an' rest. There's coffee on the stove.'

'I could use some, Mike. But let's get Valdés over here.'

'Sure, if you say so.'

Ventura stepped from the saddle and, with a nod, followed the nester past the house to an enclosed barn, the double doors of which sported a haft and staple fastening, secured by a huge padlock.

In a moment Santeely had unbarred the doors, and in the light from a hanging lantern, indicated the inconspicuous opening into the loft. Quickly he placed a ladder in position and held it steady as Ventura ascended and swung the trapdoor inwards. Here a hooded lantern hung from the ridge-pole, casting a single ghostly shaft of light onto the now pale, stubbled face of

Esteban Valdés.

'Take it easy,' Ventura told him as he climbed inside and cut the rawhide thongs securing Valdés' ankles. 'Soon as you can walk easy we're going over to the house an' talk. Mebbe it's still not too late to do some good.' He regarded Esteban curiously as the man began easing some of the stiffness from legs and feet. The contrast between his earlier vociferous protests and this present sober mood encouraged Ventura in the belief that Valdés' attitude might even now have changed sufficiently for broaching the plan he had in mind...

In the lamplit living-room the two men faced each other across the table while Santeely filled three cups with hot coffee.

'I – I guess I was pretty sore when you took me the other night, Ventura.' Valdés admitted. 'There were all kinds of – ideas – and suspicions floating around inside my head, and I still haven't been able to figure out your reasons, nor what part Santeely here is playing.

'But I'll tell you right off,' he continued earnestly, 'I never was so pleased to see anyone as I was when you appeared through that loft door just now!'

Ventura was more puzzled than he showed. He said: 'You sure have a strange way of showing pleasure, Esteban.'

Santeely planked the coffee cups down

and pushed a bowl of sugar across the table. His actions were automatic; his mind engrossed with the mystery. 'I don't get it,' he growled.

'Can I have my hands free, an' smoke?' Valdés asked, and gave a pinched-off, weary smile. 'Don't worry; I'm not figuring on trying to make a break!' Silently Ventura untied his wrists, pushed sack and papers across the table and waited while the Starcross man somewhat clumsily rolled and lit a smoke.

'I've had a deal of time since bein' here to do some thinking,' he said. 'Straight thinking this time, I reckon.' His glance lifted to their faces. 'Since you called me Steve Crow, night before last, mebbe you know something of this Señor Crow's activities, huh?'

'I know he's a new member of the Butler gang,' Ventura returned quickly, 'but, so far, luckily for him, there's no wanted notice been posted. That means the law has no record of such a hombre. It means, Valdés, if he's got any sense, he'll quit now while he's still clean...'

'Wait a minute!' The man held up his hand. 'You don't have to try and convince me. I already said there'd been plenty of time for straight thinking, and I see now I've been a fool as well as a criminal.' Just for a moment his eyes lowered and the next words seemed almost as if they were addressed to himself. 'There were reasons, though, strong reasons why I joined in with Butler.' He shrugged, drew frowningly on his cigarette. 'I said just now I was darn glad to see you, Ventura, and naturally, you wondered why! Well, let me tell you that Torch and Jim Butler have got you lined up for an early death! Sure! This thing's been on my mind for some time. I wanted to warn you, yet it was through me they heard about you, and now, if – when they send someone to get you, then–'

'Didn't you realise when you tied in with a bunch like that, it wouldn't stop at robbing? Folks are liable to get killed, most gen'rally innocent folks. It dam' near happened at Plata. Next time, likely it will!'

Valdés' eyes widened as he regarded the bounty hunter in astonishment. 'Here I've as good as admitted complicity in – in your murder, Señor, yet you do not so much as bat an eyelid?'

Ventura smiled. 'They already tried. I guess Torch and Jim Butler don't believe in wasting time over things like that. As it turned out, they sent the wrong man.'

'You – you mean you – managed to kill him?'

'No. We exchanged shots is all. I got a leg graze, no more; but Bob Ferris took a slug in the arm.'

'So! They sent Ferris after you? I saw him once hit a jack rabbit at seventy-eighty yards. I...' Valdés spread his hands as though in a gesture of defeat. 'I guess I wasn't figuring they would move quite so fast. Well, you got Ferris then, and maybe the reward?'

Ventura shook his head, reached for his cup and swallowed the coffee. 'He was clean, like you, Esteban. Lucky, too, I guess. Right now he's on his way to another county. He's broken with this ruffian life for good!'

'By hickory!' Santeely gasped. 'You take these things calmly, *amigo!* First James, thereby saving my life, to say nothing of your own; then another shooting, and this time you let the culprit go!'

'So would you have done, under the circumstances, Mike. You're no more a cold-blooded murderer than I am. Sometimes there's no alternative to killing, as in the case of James. Here things were a mite different; in fact, years back I knew this Bob Ferris under a different handle. He'd had some bad breaks – besides which he also had what you could call a change of heart – like Steven here. Now I know something I've been after discovering for a long time!'

'You mean,' Valdés said slowly, 'he talked? Well now, listen, *amigo.* I, too, am talking and I, too, am through with this – this degrading way of trying to stave off–'

208

'You needn't worry over losing Starcross, I reckon, or anything that goes with it. For a start off, Roy Holman's hazing three hun'ed an' thirty prime steers onto your land tomorrow, to replace those he had the Fletcher skunks poison! Soon as we can sell them for cash that eleven hun'ed dollars you – huh – borrowed, can be sent anonymously to the sheriff at San Pablo. He'll see it goes back to Plata's Bank!'

They stared back at Ventura in a silence that ran on unbrokenly until the Starcross owner cleared his throat and tried, awkwardly at first, to speak what was in his mind.

'I don't know how *anyone* could force Holman to do such a thing, and admit– But if you say so, Ventura, then I believe you. But that's not all. Right at the beginning I saw you only as a danger to me and my scheme for saving Starcross. That was why I told the Butlers you had captured Hank Dillis. Afterwards, when I got back and talked with my sister, I – I found out something that made me wish on the Blessed Virgin Mary I could undo the harm I had already done!' He dropped the cigarette butt into a saucer, mashing the ember with a calloused thumb. 'I guess it wouldn't have worried me much,' he went on in a low voice, 'if you'd been killed, Ventura. You were just a bounty hunter, so

209

everyone figured, out for a fast buck. Fact was, of course, if the Butlers were going to go on working this territory, with me joining in when I got the chance, then it was pretty obvious you *had* to be taken care of!' He moved his head slowly from side to side, contradicting the thought before utterance. 'It's not what you've just told me, though, about getting the cattle replaced and – and giving Starcross a chance to pull through. No…' Valdés swallowed hard. 'But this alone is enough to make me realize I've dragged our name in the mud, that I'm guilty of the dirtiest kind of trick–' He broke off and brooded a moment in silent bitterness, and then his glance came up squarely, meeting Ventura's steady gaze. 'How do you think I felt, *amigo,* when Judith told me on my return from Torch Butler's place *that you were the man she loved…?*'

CHAPTER XII

'STEVE'S SOLD HIS STORY!'

Santeely got up and fed fresh wood to the stove, and Valdés built himself another cigarette and in silence pushed the makings across the table.

210

'How can you be sure?'

Ventura knew, as he spoke, it was the kind of damn stupid question a man always asks when there seems little else to say.

Esteban's twisted smile, the typically Spanish gesture, as almost imperceptibly his shoulders lifted, only seemed to endorse his next words.

'Señor! A woman's lips often lie, her eyes seldom, if ever. But, how can I face my sister again? Already she has become–'

'She knows,' Ventura said softly. 'Some of it she began to guess at. I filled in the blanks as far as I could.'

'Then?'

'Listen! To set this thing right, are you willing to risk mebbe even more than when the Plata Bank was robbed?'

'Risk?' Valdés pushed back his chair and stood up. 'Risk?' he repeated and laughed. 'Show me any way to come out of this without dishonour, even if it means – death, and you'll find me ready! Even now it means just that, if Butler discovers who I am. And what of the risk when robbing a bank? Why, maybe on the very next job–'

'That's what I was comin' to,' the other murmured. 'If you know the details, the set-up, you can still do your share and more, but not in the way the Butler gang'll be figuring!'

Ventura studied the Starcross owner, seeing before him a man not entirely devoid of weaknesses, yet who nevertheless possessed qualities of moral as well as physical bravery in some high degree. No timid, average citizen would have had the nerve or acting ability to have done what Valdés did in the guise of Steve Crow!

Esteban licked his lips, considering the implications which lay in Ventura's words.

'The next job has been planned and everyone given their instructions,' he said quietly. 'But I – I guess I don't quite understand. Isn't it the Butler hideout you're more interested in? And another thing. What are they going to do when Ferris doesn't show up? Likely call the hold-up off, you figure?'

'Butler won't do that, not if you ride out there first thing tomorrow an' tell him you met Ferris – by accident if you like – an' told him where he could find this hombre Ventura.' The bounty hunter smiled. 'Unfortunately for Bob Ferris, there was a shoot out and Ferris was killed...'

'But–'

'...Fortunately for the Butlers, however,' he went on, '*you* were still around and were able to settle with Bob's killer! So, except that they're just one man short, they got no reason to change or cancel their plans – whatever they are!'

Valdés nodded. 'It sounds a good scheme,

and mebbe I'm beginning to see what's in back of it. If I can sell them this story, and provided nothing's altered, then I go on being Steve Crow and take part in the hold-up as planned? In a few words, we'll all be walking into a trap!'

Ventura dug down into a pocket and produced the sheriff's star which he had shown to Will Baumann a few days back. 'Here's something to convince them beyond doubt that you killed me. You went through my pockets and found this badge *and* this identification paper. Sure they'll know I was a lawman and not a drifting bounty hunter, but I'll tell you this, Esteban, it wouldn't be the first time a member of Torch Butler's gang killed a Peace Officer!'

The Starcross owner let go a deep breath. 'They're a worse bunch of *mal hombres* than I had them figured for,' he muttered, carefully pocketing the badge and document. He returned to his chair at the table as Santeely stepped across from the stove to refill the cups.

'The job, Ventura, is holding up the San Pablo stage at a certain point between the county seat and Roxburgh. Butler's information is that it'll be carrying a gold shipment close to seventy thousand dollars! But we haven't got much time. Today is, let me see, Saturday, and the shipment is scheduled for the mid-week run on Wednesday!'

213

Santeely leaned his hands on the table and addressed Ventura earnestly. 'Look, *amigo*, lawman or not, you are goin' to need all the help you can muster, so you can count me in.'

'Thanks, Mike. But very soon now I'll be layin' my cards on the table, face up. This is no longer a one-man job – if it ever was...' he grinned. 'No. Baumann and Kirby will be in on this and mebbe we can get a few others. How many men are workin' this job, Steven?'

Valdés drew a hand down his stubbled jaw. 'Here's the whole thing,' he told them grimly. 'We all meet at a place called Crooked Creek an hour before noon. There'll be six of us, on account Butler says the coach'll have a special shot-gun guard along. When we're all met, Torch will give us a few last-minute details, then we light out for the hold-up spot, the idea being to get there well ahead of time.

'The stage is due along this stretch at around three to three-thirty, but Butler figures it smart to be there early, just in case of any last-minute hitches. But, wait, *amigos,* this is not all! A man called the Deacon – he's closer to the Butlers than the rest – will then ride out to a look-out point already selected and watch the road through glasses! As soon as he's sure the stage is on its way he'll high-tail it back and warn Torch and the rest. At the right moment they'll jump the coach and shoot the lead horses...' Valdés gulped. 'That's bad enough, but not so bad as – as shooting men...' He glanced quickly at Ventura. 'I – I guess you were right when you said things don't end with stealing! If the driver or guard attempt any resistance, well, I'm beginning to see that Torch isn't likely to show them mercy.'

'He couldn't afford to, Steve, from his point of view. Not if it means losing the gold or risking the lives of his gang!'

'Sure. I – I don't know whether they figure on robbing any passengers or not. I guess that's one of the details to be ironed out on Wednesday, but each man has got a particular job to perform so's the hold-up will go smooth and quick. The gold box is the thing they're interested in, and I heard that the Deacon and Ferris have been picked to handle that, while Mackinlay, Scheche and – er – Steve Crow, cover the passengers and keep a look-out generally. Meanwhile, Torch is right there in front watching things like a hawk!'

'You've already given six names, Steve, without mentioning Jim Butler!'

'That's right. He is really the brains as far as I can make out, and seemingly doesn't usually ride, though he did at Plata –to watch *me!* But when they learn about Ferris, then maybe Jim Butler will ride in his place.'

'I see. And after the hold-up?'

'The same pattern as before. Each man has got a hideout some place, like Dillis had, or else, like me, he's able to shelter behind some respectable front!' Valdés coloured, continuing on in a low voice. 'They aim to blow the box open – Torch'll see to that – and pile the gold and any paper money into sacks. Once they've put the coach out of action long enough to give them a few hours' start, then they'll make the same play as before, confusing the trail and using creeks and streams to make pursuit dam' near impossible. Then, next Friday or Saturday, the lesser members like myself, Mackinlay and maybe even Ferris are to make their way to the sheep-farm as before, pick up their five per cent and any further instructions.

'So,' Valdés concluded, 'you know just about as much as I do now and I'm ready for whatever you want, Ventura. Mebbe – if I get – killed, it's going to save a deal of trouble for Judith…'

'Don't be a fool! You never did start this thing on your own for personal gain. Right from the beginning you were working under my instructions, for the United States Government!' As he spoke he withdrew a second badge from a concealed pocket under his belt. He held it out for their inspection.

'This is the one that counts; the one I gave you, Steve, was used many years back!'

'United States Marshal!' Santeely breathed. 'Then why...?'

Ventura smiled thinly. 'But a man's got to be sure of his lawmen first; and second, he's got to be mighty sure, before he jumps, that the evidence'll stick!'

'It seems like the Valdés are heavily in your debt, Ventura.'

'And that makes two of us!' Santeely thrust forward over the table. 'I haven't told him yet, *amigo*... He turned from one to the other. 'Two nights back, Valdés, a few hours before you were brought here, Holman sent Gil James to kill me. But–'

Ventura gestured impatiently with his hand. 'You both talk of being in debt! Why, it would've taken years mebbe to get as near to Butler as we are now, through you. Nor could I've gotten along without Santeely's help the last few days. So let's quit the back-slapping and get down to cases.'

It was late afternoon the following day when he rode slowly into Starcross. The soft-droning quiet of a Sabbath day hung lazily on the air, and despite obvious signs of weariness, Ventura experienced a strange, almost indefinable feeling of peace. Perhaps it was because he could see the end of this particular chore in sight. Or maybe it was an

217

understandable reaction to so much planning and activity of late. The results of his long journey to Fort Frazer today were alone sufficient cause for quiet satisfaction. He smiled thinly to himself as Charlie Williams stepped out from behind the bunkhouse and bow-legged his way forward, knuckling sleep from his heavy eyes.

Yes, all those things had their marked effect, yet the real answer he knew now, lay in the realization of something infinitely more precious than the mere accomplishment of mundane things alone...

'Howdy, Mr Ventura!'

Williams grinned as he came up and took the reins. 'Kinda quiet around hyar today, wouldn't you say?'

'Don't tell me Glen Summers has got the crew sweatin' on range work?'

'Wal, you might find this hard of believin,' *amigo,* but along about noon, four-five Arrow riders come in, hazin' along a herd – over three hun'ed head of prime stuff – wal, I shore didn't believe when Holman rode over last evening an' told us–'

'So! Holman came here yesterday an' said he was makin' good the trail-herd you lost?'

'Yeah!' Charlie pushed back his hat and stared at Ventura. 'But I shore don't savvy how *you* figgered it out! Reckon it beats all hell, anyways, 'cos I allus had Holman elected for the dirty coyote as planted them

Fletcher bustards onto Glen.'

'You think Glen Summers hired them in all innocence?'

'I do now, though I don't mind tellin' you I had my suspicions of Glen fer a long whiles.' The oldster moved back a pace as Ventura stepped from the saddle. 'I ain't so sure now about anythin', 'ceptin' one-two things bin said lately as makes me figger Summers hired them hombres like you said, all innocent that they were thievin', killin' polecats!'

'And what about Holman replacing the herd? Why d'you figger he's doin' this, Charlie?'

A scowl spread over the wrangler's leathery face. 'Reckon it ain't any secret he's bin makin' up to Miss Judith fer a long while an' mebbe he figgered she'd be so grateful–' He stopped and glanced towards the house, then back to Ventura. 'I ain't in the habit o' shootin' off my mouth, but Miss Judith she – wal I guess you don't 'pear like a stranger to us! Miss Judith says yo're helpin' the *jefe* with some kinda deal...?'

Ventura nodded. 'You might call it that, Charlie. I only hope it will work out right.' He caught sight of her in the open doorway, and began walking across to the house, more deeply aware of her expressive loveliness now, perhaps, than at any moment since their first meeting.

'So it *is* you this time, *amigo!* I heard a rider come in, and voices, but then so I did last evening and' – she smiled up at him – 'it was not you at all, but Roy.'

'Charlie was just telling me Holman sent over a herd this morning, kinda replacing the one that was destroyed, I guess! So mebbe that was why he called yesterday, to tell you?'

The deep blue eyes regarded him half-searchingly for a moment. 'Maybe you would care to sit out on the *patio* for a while this beautiful evening?'

He followed her into the house, through to the wide french doors at the far end that opened onto a flagged *patio* of Spanish-Pueblo design. Brick-edged plant beds had been laid out at intervals, and varieties of vividly coloured *yucca*, flowering shrubs and smaller flowers lent an incredible brilliance to the backcloth of sage-green foliage and white, adobe walls.

The scent of lupins, wild hop, yarrow, geraniums, drifted on the warm breeze, mingling with the orris perfume in Judith's glistening hair.

'Yes,' she answered when they were seated. 'I cannot really understand it, this absolute *insistence* on Roy's part to – as he described it – "make good Starcross's loss in a neighbourly way!"' She smiled, and quickly lowered her gaze. 'Of course, I know that despite everything lately he hopes – he thinks that by such means...'

'Sure. I guess I know what you mean, Judith, but – well, I can tell you now most of what's been going on behind the scenes. All I know, anyway.' He paused a moment, a slight smile quirking his lips.

'Likely Holman didn't figger I'd mention this to you, Judith, but it kinda ties in, in a way, with other things.' He told her then of how Arrow had planned the destruction of their herd, believing that with disaster staring Starcross in the face, she, Judith, would capitulate and so let Holman achieve a twofold conquest, which would further aid his plans on the climb to supreme political power.

She listened, pale-faced and silent as Ventura described in terse words how Mike Santeely had accidentally witnessed the Fletcher killings and thus had been marked down for ultimate destruction himself. Many things which had been obscure, or seen as through a misty window, now revealed themselves to Judith Valdés as the lawman went on to explain his own part in all this and why it had been decided he should masquerade as a bounty hunter.

'So you – you are really working for the Federal Government, together with this Major Arlen, your friend, in Santa Fe?'

He nodded. 'I guess mebbe we're amongst

the first of the regular Law Enforcement Officers to be given such an assignment. You see, both Holman and the Butler brothers have got criminal records, and their trails 've crossed enough times in the past to make us figger they were likely tied in together down here.

'But, in fact, it seems pretty certain now they're not working together, mebbe never did. Holman's quit petty thievin' an' such like, as his ambitions 've grown. Sure, he's just as much a killer now as when he usta pull the trigger himself.

'We know he has been responsible for at least two deaths down here, and also that he sicced Gil James onto Santeely.' He shook his head slowly. 'None of it could be proved, not even the poisoning of your trail-herd. But there's somethin' else, Judith, I've got to tell you. Esteban's working with me now, unofficially, and he rode out at dawn today, to pay Torch Butler a visit!'

'Do you mean...?'

'They'd planned another job,' he told her quietly, 'and Steve's goin' through with it, only *this* time he's workin' on the side of the law...'

'What you are trying to tell me, *amigo,* is that – that Steve is perhaps playing an even more dangerous game than before?'

'There's always a risk,' he admitted soberly. 'We'll know better when he gets back tonight.' He went on to give a word-sketch of the plan for rounding up the notorious Butler gang, a scheme which he had yet to discuss and finalize with Marshal Baumann.

Suddenly Judith arose, placed her hand on Ventura's arm. 'All this time you have given me this important news and yet I have not offered you so much as a glass of tequila. Come, Ventura, I will show you Esteban's room. There you can wash the trail dust away and refresh yourself, and afterwards you will please partake of some refreshment, *si*...?'

Dusk merged into night, and on the *patio*, wrought-iron lanterns gleamed brightly yellow, reflecting onto silver and china-ware set on the table.

Ventura rolled a quirly, and as he raised the match Judith watched the strong play of light and shadow on the dark-skinned face. There was a velvet softness in her eyes as she thought about the things he had said, particularly regarding the role he had assigned to Esteban, cleverly intimating that all along he and Steve had been working together, leaving it lay there.

Chair legs scraped on the flagstones and he rose to his feet, reaching for his hat.

'I'll haveta be goin', Judith, an' see Baumann. Thanks for the meal – for everythin'...'

Together they walked around the side of the house and along beside the adobe wall, and Judith called in her low, clear voice and in a moment Charlie's answering shout came to them through the starlit night. Down by the shadow-enveloped outbuildings a lantern gleamed, a yellow eye winking in the darkness, and then it was gone.

'The boys are late back,' Ventura murmured. 'Mebbe Summers is fixin' to get them all branded, you reckon, Judith?'

'He was hoping to do that, but I told him there was no immediate hurry.' She gestured faintly with her hands. 'We have to find a buyer yet. It may take a little time.'

They turned as Williams loomed towards them from across the yard, leading the cared-for steel-dust, and Ventura took the reins and swung up into the saddle. 'I almost forgot,' he said. 'Talking of sellin' the herd...' He withdrew an envelope from his saddle pouch and handed it down to the girl. He was quick to neck-rein the gelding, as with a soft 'Adios' he gently spurred away...

Charlie was surprised to be called again so soon, and wonderingly he followed Miss Judith into the house where she silently handed him a folded piece of foolscap paper. He had seen and handled paper like this before. It was army issue, the kind on which the Fort Frazer beef contracts were invariably drawn up. He smoothed the paper out and read the main points, stumbling over many of the words, but understanding well enough their purport. He looked up and grinned widely, and figured how strange it was the way some folks always cried when they got good news...

In the marshal's office, behind locked doors, the four men were grouped round the table. In front of them lay a detailed map of the county, and from time to time, Marshal Baumann placed a neat pencilled cross to mark some particular spot, decided upon by mutual agreement.

The air was thick with smoke and stale with the closeness of body heat. Yet attention to the business in hand was too strongly concentrated for any of the room's occupants even to notice.

'What about the passengers?' Baumann asked, glancing up from a pad on which he had been writing. 'We're all agreed there ain't much chance of arrangin' fer a decoy coach in time.'

'I reckon they'll haveta take their chance, Will.'

'But – supposin' they's wimmen ridin' that Roxburgh stretch? Cain't we git Digby to bundle all passengers out at San Pablo; fix 'em up at the hotel an' wait?'

'Supposin' one or more of them decide to hire mounts, mebbe rather than wait three days for the next stage?'

'Likely they'd take the same road,' Santeely put in, 'and sure enough the Butler gang'd figger somethin' had gone wrong!'

'I think Mike's right,' Ventura said quietly. 'It's a loophole which they might easily slip through.'

'Wal...' Baumann pulled at his drooping moustache. 'Mebbe yo're right. But it's ten to one I'd say that anyone'd be quick enough off the mark to git a hoss an' pound the stage road *ahaid* of the coach. Besides which, if there was no passengers–'

'I know what you're thinkin', Will,' Ventura smiled. 'Three-four of us could've bundled in an' mebbe shot it out with the bandits when they attacked! Frankly, Will, I'm scared the Butlers are gonna smell a rat if things aren't just like they should be. Plen'y times before they slipped through our hands on account of playin' some hunch or bein' tipped off by the chance remark of some innocent bystander.' He leaned forward over the table. 'Like I told you, Steve's bin pretty smart workin' at this: playing a part, gettin' himself taken on by Torch, and now bringing back just the information we've been waiting for.

'There's this hombre known as the Deacon. He's their first lieutenant and, like

226

the two brothers, is wanted from Dodge to Tucson, but for none of 'em had we got a real description until Steve was able to supply it.'

'You rate this Deacon as dangerous as Torch an' Jim Butler?' Ollie Kirby suggested.

Ventura nodded. 'Sure. And here's the point I'm tryin' to make. Steve says the Deacon is look-out man on this job. He'll be watchin' the road through glasses in good time to warn them when the coach appears. *He could decide to ride clear into San Pablo, gentlemen, and smell things out!*' He paused long enough to roll and light a quirly. In the thick silence the striking of the match sounded like a small explosion.

'That's what he did before the Plata job, didn't you say?' It was Kirby who put the question.

'Yeah. But we hadn't gotten any descriptions at that time,' Ventura put in quickly. 'Steve had only seen Torch Butler, and that in a badly-lit room. From what is known now, it seems the Deacon looked the town over, bold as paint. If he should try the same thing at San Pablo...' Ventura's hand sliced the air in an expressive gesture.

'Yo're sayin' that could be another way of them findin' out about the coach an' passengers?' Baumann grunted. 'Yeah, I guesso. But what about wisin' up the drivers an' guard? Cain't–?'

'Ah, Will, that's somethin' we'll surely do both for their sakes and the travellers'. A warning like that might well save injuries, mebbe lives. Something that can be done without attracting any attention.'

They nodded agreement, and Kirby got up and for the first time seemed to notice the smoke and fumes. He opened the top half of the window and tramped across to the stove, peered at the warming coffee and made his inevitable inquiry of the others.

For the third time within the last hour the marshal's glance lifted to the clock, seeing the crawling hands pointed at a quarter of nine.

'When you figure he'll be back?' Baumann had asked the question before, much earlier. Maybe he had forgotten; more likely he remembered well enough and hoped Ventura might be more encouraging now.

'You've seen roughly where the farm is, Will, on this map. He was gone over ten hours, I guess, takin' out from Starcross. It's that much further from Mike's place.'

'He left dam' early this mornin',' Santeely growled, 'same as you did, Ventura. Bin gone near to sixteen hours!'

'If he don't show up soon,' Baumann said softly, 'we'll haveta fergit about Wednesday's coach an' organize a posse to–'

Above the bustle of evening traffic the

228

sounds of a single rider came through the half-open window. Unmistakably, the horse had been reined in right outside, and three men remained transfixed as Ventura reached the door, unlocked it and swung it wide.

A moment's breathless pause as he stepped onto the boardwalk and narrowed his eyes against the conflict of bright light and deep shadow. Then he turned back into the office, smiling.

'Steve's sold his story!' he told them, and felt the tension leave his body in a long, gusty sigh…

CHAPTER XIII

LUCK FIGURES IN EVERYTHING

One of the main essentials for the ultimate success of Ventura's plan, as in any such undertaking, was absolute secrecy. Too often a chance word carelessly dropped by a deputy or posse man would, like a burning match on dry brush, touch off a blaze sufficient to warn the criminals, giving them both the time and opportunity to beat a fast retreat.

Not only this, but it was necessary for men like the marshal and Ventura – men in the public eye – to avoid any suggestion of unusual activity or deep-laid purpose.

And though Valdés had obtained the vital information to make this ambush-trap possible, had even convinced the Butlers of Ventura's death, there were still several details which the outlaw leader had not supplied for obvious reasons.

Steven had said that in the beginning both the brothers received his story with more than a mite of suspicion, especially Jim Butler. Only when he had calmly pulled Ventura's law-badge from his pocket, together with money and papers, had the atmosphere changed abruptly. His final and convincing trick had been in assuring the desperadoes that the shooting had occurred in open country with no witnesses around and that he, Steve Crow, had been smart enough to catch up both horses and send them, along with their erstwhile owners, to the bottom of a precipitous gorge.

Thus, on the Monday morning, Ventura had ridden slowly out of town, with every appearance of a man engaged in nothing more deadly than the casual exercise of himself and his mount. And later, at a lonely spot on the trail to San Pablo, Marshal Will Baumann joined him. A good deal of that day, as far as the two lawmen were concerned, was spent closeted with Sheriff Digby and a few special deputies in a private office of San Pablo's courthouse. By the afternoon the plan had been covered from all possible angles and the men under Digby detailed for their particular jobs.

The following evening four men were ready to ride out from Latigos once more, or nearly so. It only remained for Mike Santeely to make his appearance, and at eight o'clock sharp, his face somewhat taut, the Jarvis strip nester walked into Baumann's office and closed the door behind him.

Ventura eyed him carefully, knowing where he had been, beginning to understand more, something of this man's obstinate adherence to any kind of self-conceived principle.

Baumann's glance flickered from one to the other, but it was to Kirby he spoke.

'Everythin' ready at Nimrod's?'

'Sure. Hosses, canteens, rifles...'

'Better pack a few more Winchester slugs, Ollie. Take a coupla boxes from the drawer an' wait at the livery, huh?'

Kirby nodded, helped himself to the .44 ammunition and, with a short nod, stepped from the room.

'Look, Mike,' Ventura said softly. 'For heaven's sake! You don't haveta take this on yourself. Me an' Will an' Kirby – well, it's our job, isn't it? We–'

'Save it,' Santeely said flatly. 'I've allus bin

a fool; why try stoppin' me now?' He regarded the two men quizzically, yet with a self-derisive gleam in his eyes. 'Like you told me, I didn't let on to Dulcie what was happenin'. Told her I'd got to attend to some business that might keep me away sometime! I guess I've never hated lyin' so much in all my life, but—'

'It was either that, Mike, or not see her at all. You understand...'

'Sure I do! But it's hell lyin' to the woman you love, 'specially when you're not sure you'll be comin' back!'

'Hell!' Baumann grunted, 'it ain't gonna be like that Santeely.'

'Mebbe not. Mebbe at that, it made me feel good deep down inside when – when she kissed me.' A sudden change was in his voice and a soft light in his eyes. 'I know now – dam' me fer a fool, I should 'a' known well enough before...'

'What about her hus – this hombre Fredericks?' Baumann asked curiously. 'Wasn't he figgerin' on comin' to Latigos?'

Santeely nodded and shifted the unaccustomed gun at his hip to a more comfortable position. 'Still is as far as we know.' He shrugged. 'As Ventura would say, *quién sabe?* Mebbe it's the bustard's idea of a joke. But – hell! You don't wanta hear about such things, an' besides, it's nigh on time we was movin'.'

232

'May as well finish it now, Mike,' Ventura drawled. 'I've got a kinda interest in all this, y'know, since I followed that buckboard's trail.'

'There isn't anythin' to tell, I guess. Just that Dulcie is – wal, she figgers when Fredericks does show up, she – wal the both of us together that is, are gonna let the whole town know everythin', kinda forestall Mr Samuel Fredericks…'

'I like that,' Will Baumann said grinning. 'I like that a whole lot. Might even end in Miss Dulcie gettin' a divorce an – everythin'!'

'Time for you and Ollie to drift, Will,' Ventura said. 'See you in San Pablo…'

The sun climbed higher in a steely blue sky, drawing moisture from the land and sweat from the pores of men's bodies.

From around nine-thirty this morning the lawmen and a few specially deputized citizens had been waiting on either side the stage road to Roxburgh, some two-three miles from Crooked Creek. It was a boring, monotonous business, this waiting, and once or twice Ventura heard muttered protests from a couple of the San Pablo men.

Yet it had been essential to get here with plenty of time in hand. There was no knowing at exactly what hour the Butler gang might show up. All Steve had been able to say was that they were to meet at Crooked Creek an hour before noon. It might take an hour or two to finalize their plans; it could be done in a matter of minutes.

From Ventura's point of view it wasn't so easy to figure all the angles, to cover every possibility with only ten men, seven of whom were virtual strangers; and it had taken more than a little discussion last night before Sheriff Digby had reluctantly agreed to play it Ventura's way.

For the third time this morning Ventura climbed down from a high, piñon-dotted upthrust of rocks, a battered pair of glasses in his hand. Below, in a narrow fissure, Baumann and Santeely waited with Jake Rawlins and Herbert Daler, two of Digby's men.

'No sign as yet, but then the view's not so clear as from Ollie's side of the road.'

Mike Santeely drew a turnip watch from his vest pocket.

'Half after noon, *amigo*,' he began and then, clear across from a high promontory seven hundred yards away, came Ollie Kirby's single heliograph flash.

'Someone's on the way,' Ventura said quietly. 'Either the whole gang or mebbe just the Deacon to scout the road ahead.' He turned to one of the deputies. 'Pass the word to the sheriff, Rawlins, to get his men under cover.'

'Okay.' Rawlins made his way from the rock fissure, crossed the road quickly and disappeared into the further brush-skirted boulders and sandstone croppings.

He was back inside of fifteen minutes, and almost on his heels came Ollie Kirby, face alight with excitement. 'It's them all right, Mr Ventura! Six of 'em, jest like Steve said. Could see 'em clear enough through the glasses till they hit the brush–'

'Good work, Ollie! Now get back up there fast an' soon as you see one of 'em break for cover an' head across country, don't signal, just come a-runnin'!'

Kirby nodded and hurried off.

'Those hosses all right, Will?'

'They were an hour ago, but it might be a good idea if Daler here was to watch 'em.'

'Go to it, Herb, will you?' Ventura said and turned back to the others. It struck Will Baumann that this was the first time he had seen the Federal man looking a mite anxious.

'There ain't anythin' else we kin do, *amigo*, not till we get a signal. Quit worryin'!'

Ventura smiled. 'Who said I was worrying? Mebbe I was just thinkin' about Lennox the driver, an' the shot-gun guard – what was his name – Phil Lovington?'

'Yeah. Both reliable men. So's Bill Horton, the deppity Digby left behind to warn 'em!'

'Sure. He stacked up. Thank God, anyway, there's no wimmenfolk travellin' beyond San Pablo today.' He shook his head. 'I still wish we could've warned them, though. Mebbe—' He stopped short at the sound of boots slithering on rock and saw Kirby running towards the fissure opening.

He was short on breath and perspiring plenty, otherwise he seemed surprisingly happy.

'Saw him ride off 'bout twen'y minutes back!' he burst out. 'Musta bin the Deacon, I reckon. Tall feller dressed in black an' ridin' a white-stockinged sorrel horse!'

'So far everythin's goin' like we figgered, an' I sure hope it stays that way. Will! Who's the look-out man on Digby's side?'

'Deputy Sheriff Spooner.'

'All right! I'm going out to keep an eye on him and watch when he moves.'

'We'll wait right here for you,' Baumann said.

Ventura found a rock shelf some two-three hundred yards along, adequately screened from the road by straggling brush and piñon, yet in full view of the deputy, perched higher up over the other side. Link Spooner had been selected as the main look-out on account of his remarkable eye-sight and instinct for such things. According to Digby and Baumann, too, there wasn't much that Spooner missed even to the smallest movement over a wide area.

Almost as soon as Ventura had reached his perch, Spooner swung his gaze round and down over the road and across to the brush and rocks opposite. He lifted his hand very slightly in the prearranged signal, and returned to his task of watching for the Deacon's return.

It seemed to Ventura, squatting out there in the very minimum of shade, that not only was this the hottest day yet, but by far the longest! He began considering the alternative ways this grim game might have been played, worrying a little now, that for sake of the thousand-to-one chance of tipping the Butlers off, he had insisted that all coach passengers must be kept in ignorance of what lay ahead for them on the Roxburgh road. Only Buster Lennox and Phil Lovington were to be warned by the San Pablo man, Horton. Maybe he should have tried fixing for a decoy coach loaded with armed men! Maybe he should have told the Express Agent to hold all the passengers—His thoughts were interrupted suddenly by the quick sweeping movement of Spooner's arm. A moment later the deputy was descending from his eyrie, disappearing every now and again behind rock walls and screening foliage. No more did Ventura consider the things he might have done. There was only room now for following the irrevocably chosen course. He clambered down, jumped the last six feet, and came on towards the rock fissure at a dead run.

But Baumann was already at the opening and turned quickly at sight of the Federal man running.

'Ollie! Get Daler and the hosses!'

A few moments later Ventura hauled up at the hideout, his quick glance sweeping over Baumann, Santeely and Rawlins.

'Spooner's given the high sign all right! But it may be a while yet...'

'Seems like they might be cutting things a leetle fine,' Mike Santeely observed, tugging out his watch. 'If this thing isn't runnin' fast with excitement, I'd say the time was nearly three-fifteen.'

Ventura nodded and wiped some of the sweat from his neck. 'In any case, we gotta give Spooner at least twen'y minutes to reach Digby.'

'He musta had more'n half that time by now,' Baumann said and swung round as Daler and Kirby came up with the horses. In a matter of seconds the six men were in their saddles and from somewhere down the stage road, beyond the bend, came the faint crack of a pistol-shot.

'They musta moved almighty fast,' Ventura muttered and pointed the steel-dust towards the hidden trail paralleling the road. It was just too bad if Spooner had not yet reached Digby, he thought, as the gelding leaped forward at the touch of spurs. For some strange reason the Deacon could only have got back minutes before the stage itself. Something must have delayed him or else—

Ventura thrust speculation aside, concentrating on the narrow trail and suddenly glimpsing a break in the wall of rock and brush to his right.

'Through here!' Baumann yelled above the rataplan of pounding hooves, and six riders wheeled, racing through the clearing to hit the hard, dusty road with a thunderous impact. Baumann and Kirby spurred forward, one on either side the steel-dust, with Santeely, Rawlins and Daler bunched close behind, and almost at once the small, grim-visaged posse was sweeping round the sharp curve ahead in a fog of rising dust and grit.

Less than a quarter-mile away the Concord stood in the middle of the road, both lead horses down, the rear teams lunging and straining at the traces, while around them masked riders curvetted their mounts, weapons gleaming in the afternoon sun, hoarse voices raised threateningly and clear despite the confining black bandanas.

So quickly had the lawmen burst upon the scene that Ventura scarcely had time to single out individuals with any hope of immediate identification. True, the blocky man astride the bay was certainly Torch Butler himself, for, as Steve had forecast, he was holding a watching brief right now, big pistol held ready as two other riders waited with a dangerous impatience for the now unarmed Lovington to throw down the box.

Even such details as these were no more than lightning impressions, for already the leader had turned at the sound of pounding hooves behind him. Four hundred yards can be covered by galloping horses in a matter of twenty or thirty seconds, and Ventura's bunch had cut the distance by over half when the chunky man aimed his gun and sent six close shots into the oncoming horsemen. Ventura's horse swerved suddenly; beside him a man fell from the saddle, and all at once the air was full of the noise of exploding guns and the reek of cordite.

The men surrounding the coach had pulled back, half-wheeled their mounts, and were firing at the new-comers. Simultaneously with this action, Phil Lovington had leaped down from the box to retrieve the shot-gun he had been forced to drop. He had his hand on the stock, finger on the trigger, when the other thickset outlaw – Jim Butler for a certainty – whirled and snapped a shot at almost zero range. Lovington's rifle dropped as blood spread quickly across the front of his shirt. He lurched back against the front wheel, but his would-be killer never had time for a second, finishing shot.

The posse men had pulled up; one or two had slid from saddles and were firing, but with extreme difficulty, from behind their cavorting mounts. Ventura's gun, already in his hand, flashed up and roared, and twenty yards or so away Jim Butler clutched at his chest and slowly slid from his horse.

And then, from across the road, beyond a curtain of scrub oak and thick brush came the fast crescendo beat of racing hooves. Until this moment it had seemed that the desperadoes would not only stand and fight, but that they had a fair chance even now of coming through not only with their lives but with seventy thousand dollars as well. Two of the six posse men were out of the fight, Rawlins for keeps and Mike Santeely at least temporarily.

So far, the odds were slightly in favour of the outlaws, and when Torch Butler glimpsed his brother's body slip from the saddle he was more than ever bitterly resolved to wipe out these tin star law hounds.

In that moment of decision, at sight of Jim's body still and bloody in the scuffed up dirt, Torch Butler dropped his empty gun and reached for the other, as several things happened simultaneously and with devastating results.

Lead was still whining fiercely, with the two opposing factions drawing away a little to seek some kind of cover, however small, as Digby and Spooner burst into view from the other side of the road. It took Torch Butler but a swift moment to see, as well as hear, that there were other riders behind the sheriff and his chief deputy.

And then, from the rear of the stationary coach, a Winchester opened up with deadly effect, ten shots levered and fired into the now close-herded riders behind Sheriff Bart Digby. The Deacon was crouched down on one knee, coolly aiming the carbine at this latest threat and, understandably, in the face of that hail of lead, Digby wheeled his mount and signalled his men to get the hell out of range. No bunch of riders, even trained and armed deputies, could be expected to hurl themselves at those fast and accurate .44 shells, and with this sudden trick by the Deacon, the other three raiders became galvanized into action.

For a few minutes it seemed that Torch Butler and his men might still get away with it, despite a disparity in numbers. For these men were fighting now for their very lives. The chances of escape were small; whichever way they looked they saw only a glinting gun-barrel or the gallows ahead…

Chance, luck, the unforeseen incident – these things so often play a part at such a climactic moment. And now, in the dust and heat of this as yet unresolved and bitter fight, with men down on both sides, the coach door swung violently open and a tall, black-garbed figure lurched out, long-barrelled gun in his hand, as he stood there a moment, swaying with the foolish uncertainty of a man half-liquored, yet still in his unhurried way capable of surprising things. Behind him, in the coach, white faces peeped from the window as with drunken deliberation the tall man aimed and fired straight at the Deacon's back. The reloaded carbine slithered from the bandit's grasp as he pitched over on his face, and at the same moment Mackinlay raised his gun, viciously firing three shots straight off into the drunken man's body. And then, like a pack of cards blown down in a draught of wind, all resistance crumpled, as with a hoarse shout Torch Butler spurred his mount along the road, calling on his remaining henchmen to run the gauntlet of the lawmen's guns.

So quickly was the signal given and the fight broken off, that for a few dazed seconds the scattered posse men could only stare dazedly through the curtain of rising dust and swirling gun-smoke. Mackinlay, Schecke and Torch Butler were crowding in on Steve, making his chances of escape now more slender even than before.

Faintly, above the din of racing hooves and exploding guns Valdés heard a man shout, *'Don't shoot!'* But it was then too late! He felt the searing stab of pain in his back and everything misted before his eyes as he felt himself falling, falling, vainly and feebly struggling to escape the crushing iron-shod hooves about him...

In the long room, french doors wide open to the sunlit *patio*, four men sat sipping the cool drinks brought to them by a smiling Josefa.

The tall, dark-haired stranger with the penetrating yet kindly grey eyes, thoughtfully stroked his trimmed beard, glancing from one to other with a pleased smile.

'Well, gentlemen, we've managed to put an end to a bunch of desperadoes perhaps even more dangerous than the James' brothers gang. Certainly, over a period of years, Torch and Jim Butler have operated over a much wider area, robbing, murdering and causing through their brutal methods much suffering, quite apart from the considerable financial losses to banks, Express companies and individuals alike.

'I figured you would like to know, Marshal Baumann, that full credit both to you and your deputy has been acknowledged in my report, as well as to the San Pablo officials.'

Baumann shifted uncomfortably in his

chair, colouring a little, yet so obviously pleased.

'Thanks, Major Arlen, but I guess everyone–'

'Ah, but it is not always easy to get the unqualified co-operation of local Peace Officers, Marshal. Naturally enough, there are so often two opposing points of view. However–'

The door opened and Judith came in, a soft smile on her drawn face. Awkwardly the men rose, unspoken questions in their eyes, but her gaze was on Ventura as he moved across to stand beside her.

'Steve is going to be all right,' she said in a low, vibrant voice. 'The doctor is still with him. It may be a long while, but that is not important. Now, please be seated, gentlemen, and do not let me interrupt–'

'Your brother did a fine job, Miss Valdés,' Arlen said, 'and we are grateful for his help. Thankful, too, at this good news you have given us.'

'That's not the only good news, either,' Ventura told them. 'Mebbe this is something of a more personal nature, but I reckon Mike here won't mind me sayin' that very soon now the weddin' bells'll be ringing! Sure! After we got back to San Pablo on Wednesday evening, I talked to the Express Agent again. Something he said about a big, drunken fellow who kept on muttering to himself, roused my curiosity, 'specially when Nichols, the agent, said he insisted on climbing into the coach at the last moment...'

Ventura paused. 'I guess the details don't matter much, except this hombre figured he was riding on the stage to Latigos and not Roxburgh. Well,' he smiled, turning to Santeely. 'Mebbe now you'd like to finish it, Mike.'

The nester grinned, almost sheepishly, and carefully adjusted his bandaged right arm to a more comfortable position. 'It was Sam Fredericks right enough, the husband of Miss Randell, and the man who'd made her life pretty miserable over the years.' Santeely scowled a little as, addressing himself mainly to Judith, he told briefly of the letters and blackmail threats.

'But for the fact he had been drinking heavily and climbed aboard the wrong coach, he would be in Latigos right now, causing plen'y trouble.'

'I know some of this,' Judith Valdés admitted with an understanding smile. 'You see, Mr Santeely, Miss Randell came out to see me on Tuesday night. Earlier on, she had been talking to Hatch Nimrod at the livery and saw Ollie Kirby with the four saddled horses. Only later, when she saw you ride out of town ahead of Señor Ventura and following the marshal and deputy Kirby, did

she start fearing for you and wondering –
especially after the – the Gil James affair!'

'So she came – here?'

Judith nodded and crossed the room to an
inner door, opening it and smilingly
beckoning the nester over.

'She is still here, Mr Santeely,' she said,
gently pushing him through into the other
room.

Frank Arlen climbed to his feet, bowing
gallantly to Judith. 'If you will excuse me,
Miss Valdés, there are several urgent matters
needing attention before I return to Santa
Fe. But there's one piece of news that
should interest both you and Ventura.'

'On my way here I received information
from a reliable source that Roy Holman is
selling his Arrow Spread to a cattle syndicate...'

When Major Arlen had left, Judith said. 'I
didn't think to ask *why* Holman should
suddenly decide on a thing like that–'

'Mebbe,' Baumann suggested reaching for
his hat, 'it's got somethin' to do with a
bounty hunter as shoots too fast an' too
straight fer Holman's gunslicks!'

'You mean – Gil James?' Judith asked.

'Sure. Hake Murray as well! Hake tried to
kill Ventura soon after we got back to
Latigos the next day. He was waiting up-
stairs in the Bosque House.'

'You didn't tell me!' In Judith's dark eyes

247

lay the fear of what might have been.

'Luck figgers in everythin', I guess,' Ventura murmured. 'Same as it did when we finally broke the Butler gang. In this case Hake was too eager and shot the moment I opened my room door. In the short space of time it took Murray to be sure, I was able to step back, still holding onto the door.' He smiled wearily. 'There wasn't enough time to duck right out, but at least Hake's bullet struck the inside door-knob.'

'You had to kill him?'

'He managed to wing him, is all,' Baumann put in quietly. 'Even though Murray did deserve to die – wal, mebbe I know how Ventura feels…'

The Federal man slowly unbuckled his gun-belt, dropped it onto a chair, and led Judith Valdés by the arm out onto the *patio*. 'Sometimes a gun gets too heavy to carry, Judith, but until things are different–' He stopped suddenly and held her gently at arm's length. 'Why talk about such things, anyway? Frank Arlen's fixin' some leave for me. I was wonderin'…'

She was in his arms, pressed tight against him, her face upturned and radiant beyond belief. 'Do not ever wonder or doubt, so far as our love is concerned, *querido mío*,' she whispered softly, and raised her tremulous lips to his.

The publishers hope that this book has given you enjoyable reading. Large Print Books are especially designed to be as easy to see and hold as possible. If you wish a complete list of our books please ask at your local library or write directly to:

Dales Large Print Books
Magna House, Long Preston,
Skipton, North Yorkshire.
BD23 4ND

This Large Print Book for the partially sighted, who cannot read normal print, is published under the auspices of

THE ULVERSCROFT FOUNDATION

Other DALES Titiles
In Large Print

HAZEL BAXTER
Doctor In Doubt

JEAN EVANS
The White Rose Of York

J. D. KINCAID
A Hero of the West

ELLIOT LONG
Scallon's Law

LORNA PAGE
The Nurse Investigates

SALLY SPENCER
Murder At Swann's Lake

JACQUELYN WEB
The Lonely Heart